REMEMBER

"Give me your name and phone number, and I'll call you before I leave tomorrow," he said.

"I'm Molly Donnelly," she said, and she gave him her phone number, twice.

"I'll call you Molly," he said, and he repeated her number.

She walked away quickly and glanced back once. He was watching her. She was tempted to turn and run back to him, to say something — anything — to tell him a secret to keep forever. To make him promise that she would see him again.

She stopped — and he ran toward her, holding out his arms. He swung her around, laughing, and hugging her hard enough to make her gasp.

"That's to remember me by, Molly," he said.

Molly Donnelly

JEAN THESMAN

AN AVON FLARE BOOK

AVON BOOKS
A division of
The Hearst Corporation
1350 Avenue of the Americas
New York, New York 10019

Copyright © 1993 by Jean Thesman
Published by arrangement with Houghton Mifflin Company
Library of Congress Catalog Card Number: 92-10644
ISBN: 0-380-72252-6
RL: 5.0

First Avon Flare Printing: August 1994

AVON FLARE TRADEMARK REG. U.S. PAT. OFF. AND IN OTHER COUNTRIES, MARCA REGISTRADA, HECHO EN U.S.A.

Printed in the U.S.A.

RA 10 9 8 7 6 5 4 3 2 1

This is for Sam Mallett.

1

Margaret Mary Donnelly opened her diary and pushed it into the small circle of lamplight cast on her desk. On a fresh page, she wrote:

Sunday, December 7, 1941, before church

Paul Gardner was at the movies last night, sitting with Henry Green two rows ahead of us!
We saw *The Maltese Falcon*. Uncle Charlie and I think it is the best movie ever. Mama and Dad said it was pretty good. Dusty fell asleep and snored.
Today I'll . . .

"Molly, are you coming to church with me or not?" her uncle asked through her closed door. "I've got my coat on and I'm champing at the bit."

"I'm coming," Molly called out. She turned off her desk lamp and then, remembering her brother's fascination with her diary, shoved it in its hiding place under her mattress.

In the hall, Uncle Charlie leaned against the wall with his eyes closed. "Oh, God," he groaned, "how much longer do I have to wait for this young lady? Is this a penance? Wasn't an act of contrition and three Our Fathers enough for You at confession?"

"Stop that," Molly whispered. "Don't wake everybody up by talking to God in the hall. Come on, it's seven-thirty."

She tiptoed past her parents' door and hurried down the carpeted steps to the dining room, trusting her uncle to follow her, unless he was feeling friskier than usual and planned to torment the rest of the family by banging on their bedroom doors and yelling something funny. The last time it had been, "There are apes on the roof! Giant apes from the zoo! Run!"

Dad had opened his bedroom door and shouted, "The only ape here is you, Charlie," and slammed the door shut so hard that one of his bedroom windows cracked.

Remembering, Molly grinned and looked back. Charlie was right behind her, buttoning his Sunday-best overcoat.

"You're ready at last?" he exclaimed. "We can go now? You've powdered your nose and straightened your seams?"

Twelve years old, Molly wore neither powder nor silk stockings with seams. But she was pleased that he put her in the same category with Mama. "We've got plenty of time," she told him.

They let themselves out of the house and into the winter dark. When mass was over, the sun would be up, and the world would look better. But now, the thin ice on the sidewalks glimmered in the streetlights, and the bitter wind blowing from Puget Sound clicked ominously in the bare branches overhead.

"I hate it when it's so dark in the morning," Molly complained, digging her hands deep into her pockets. She skipped a little to keep up with her uncle, who was tall and long-legged and seldom slowed down for her until she asked.

"Just two more weeks and a few days, and then we start back toward longer days and shorter nights," Uncle Charlie said. "Spring will be here before you know it. In the meantime, think about Christmas. That's cheerful enough."

"Okay," Molly said. "What are *you* giving me?"

Uncle Charlie's shouted laughter rang out in the empty street. Somewhere a dog barked and fell silent again.

"Go ahead, tell me," Molly said. "I already know what Maureen sent me."

"You do not," Uncle Charlie argued. "We haven't opened the shipping crate yet, so how can you know what your present is?"

"Because Maureen told me about it in her last letter, that's how," Molly said. "She said she'd give me an embroidered shirt and some beads made by Philippine artists. So there."

"My daughter, my very own flesh and blood, could never keep a secret to save her soul," Charlie said. "She got that from her mother. Moira told everybody everything, God rest her. Well, you won't get a hint from me about your present."

"It won't be as good as a shirt and beads from the Philippines," Molly said, to goad him. She skipped ahead of him and danced backward, laughing. "And guess what! Emily Tanaka said she's giving me something that her auntie sent from Hawaii, especially for me.

I'm getting two — no, three — things from islands this Christmas."

"Heavens, I'll have to throw out what I bought you," Charlie said. "It was only made here in Seattle. Now get out of my way and act like a girl who's on her way to church — not that they should let you in, unbaptized devil that you are."

It was true. Molly — and Dusty, too — had never been baptized. Dad had been raised Catholic like Uncle Charlie, but he had "fallen away," as Grandma Donnelly had always put it, causing Molly to think of Dad toppling helplessly off a cliff into the dark. Mama was what Grandma had called a "heathen Irish Protestant," although she never went to any church. But Molly liked church, the orderliness and the rituals, and so she went with Charlie every Sunday.

"Look," Molly said, pointing ahead to the end of the block, "there's Mr. Barrows. How come he's going to eight o'clock mass again?"

"Maybe he wants to escape from gossiping women like his wife and other people I could name," Charlie said. "Hurry a little. I want to talk shop with him."

Molly shook her head and hung back. She hated it when Charlie talked about work with Dad or Mr. Barrows or anybody else who worked for the Boeing Aircraft Company. Planes and war, war and planes. There had been too much talk of war in the last few months. In Europe, Germany's Hitler fought with everybody. In the Pacific, the Empire of Japan warred with China. Emily Tanaka, who lived next door, worried all the time that Hitler would bomb Seattle, even though their seventh grade teacher had told her at least a dozen times that Germany was too far away, and what was happening in England could not happen in Seattle.

Her uncle hailed Mr. Barrows, who stopped to wait under the corner streetlight. Molly dawdled, then trailed after them.

Ahead, she saw the shabby old church, giving forth warm, yellow light and a sort of haughty hospitality. She would have heard organ music if the ten o'clock mass was about to begin. But there was no music at the eight o'clock, which was one of the reasons Uncle Charlie liked it better. Organ music reminded him of Aunt Moira's funeral.

Uncle Charlie and Mr. Barrows had disappeared inside the church. Molly tugged open the heavy old door and followed them into the warm vestibule. The air there smelled of incense and the smoky coal furnace in the basement.

She found an empty pew and watched her uncle light a candle in front of the statue of the Virgin Mary. He had done this every Sunday since Aunt Moira died. Five years of Sundays, five years of candles flickering in the shadows under the serene marble gaze.

"Hey, Molly."

When she heard the whisper, her head whipped around so fast that her hat tilted on her head.

Paul Gardner sat down next to her, pulling his knit cap off his thick blond hair. His eyes were the color of turquoise, his lashes were sooty black.

"You come to early mass every Sunday?" he asked.

She nodded and settled her hat with both hands. Seeing

Paul anywhere but their seventh grade class had always struck her dumb.

"We don't," Paul whispered. "But we're driving to Olympia today for my grandparents' wedding anniversary, so we had to come early. But you're not even Catholic, are you?"

Molly was not certain how to answer him, but her tongue had stuck to the roof of her mouth, so all she could do was stare.

A blond woman wearing a wonderful red coat came down the aisle then, leading two small blond girls by their hands. She saw Paul sitting with Molly and hissed something at him. He got up immediately, smiling at Molly and blushing a little. Molly was so dazzled that she was afraid everybody in the church could hear her ears ring.

"See you tomorrow," he said.

Molly slid down in the pew, grinned helplessly, and rolled her eyes up. Wait until she told Emily, and Louise, her other best friend, about this!

After church, Uncle Charlie always stayed behind to have breakfast with Father O'Hara in the rectory. Father O'Hara was Aunt Moira's brother, and the two men were close friends. But Molly headed home, because her Sunday was just beginning.

She found her parents and Dusty sitting down to breakfast in the kitchen. Her brother clutched the funny papers and would have opened them over his plate, but his father said, "How many times have I told you, Dusty? No reading at the table."

Dusty whined, but he carried the papers away and returned to scowl at Molly and kick the leg of his chair, trying to annoy her.

Dusty was eight years old, but Molly was of the private opinion that he deliberately behaved like a kindergarten brat because he knew he could get away with it. He was her mother's favorite, with reddish brown hair like Mama's instead of black, like Dad's, and a scattering of freckles — a "dusting" of freckles, Mama always said. Molly looked like the Donnellys, black-haired and blue-eyed, with clear white skin.

"Hang up your coat, Molly," her mother said. "How many waffles do you want?"

"Me?" Molly asked. "Two, like always." Her cold fingers fumbled with her buttons while she hurried upstairs to put away her good coat.

She raised the window shade in her bedroom and pushed aside the curtain. There were lights on downstairs in the Tanaka house, which had once been Grandma Donnelly's. The sky was overcast, but didn't look as if it would dump rain on them that day. Not too much, anyway.

Molly hung her coat in her closet and changed into an old school skirt, almost too small now, and a shabby sweater and pair of shoes handed down from Maureen. She replaced her winter church dress on the hanger between her summer church dress and the green taffeta party dress Uncle Charlie had given her. Then, mindful of Dusty's habitual snooping, she checked on her diary and shoved it farther back under her mattress, closer to the old sock in which she hid her allowance.

Downstairs, two waffles waited for her on her plate. She sat down and reached for the syrup.

"You running off again with Emily and Louise?" her mother asked as she poured orange juice.

"We need clamshells from the beach for our science project," Molly said. "Emily's bringing stuff to eat at lunchtime."

"A picnic in this weather?" her mother asked. "I don't know what you girls see in playing around on the beach in winter."

"I'm going, too," Dusty yelled. "If there's a picnic, I'm going." In his excitement, he tipped the jam jar against his juice glass, spilling both across the table.

"Molly, let him . . . ," her mother began as she scooped up the mess with a dishtowel.

Horrified, Molly dropped her fork with a clatter. "If he comes, then the Barrows twins will too, and everything will be spoiled."

"He's your brother," her mother said, her voice flat.

"I thought Uncle Charlie was taking Dusty with him to buy the Christmas tree," Molly said, relieved that she had remembered Charlie's plans for the afternoon.

"I'd rather go with Uncle Charlie and pick out a tree than go with you and those girls," Dusty said. "I don't want to go anywhere with a Jap and a freak and a knock-kneed sister."

"Mama!" Molly cried.

"Dusty, don't say Jap again," Mrs. Donnelly warned. "And stop calling Louise a freak."

"She limps . . ."

"So would you if you'd had polio," Molly said.

She looked at her mother, hoping that she'd say something else to Dusty, scold him, punish him somehow. But her mother turned back to the waffle iron, her shoulders set. Molly's father ignored the ruckus. He wore his usual morose expression, as if the whole world tasted bad to him.

Molly had once questioned her uncle about why the brothers were so different. Uncle Charlie, much older than Molly's father, was as cheerful as his brother was unhappy.

"It's because he was born in the dark hours, when moonlight can still cast a shadow," Uncle Charlie had explained. "Now me, I was born at high noon on a sunny day, just like you, Molly Donnelly. We were blessed the moment we opened our eyes!"

Molly didn't always feel blessed, but if she'd been asked what changes she wanted in her life, she'd have said, "None!" She believed her uncle when he said, "Better the devil you know than the devil you don't."

She finished breakfast as quickly as she could without attracting Mama's attention. Mama hated to see a girl gobble her food. Just as she carried her plate to the sink, Emily knocked on the back door, and Molly waved at her through the glass panel.

"I'm going now, Mama," Molly said.

"Come back if you get too cold," her mother said.

"Hey, Molly, I'll tell Uncle Charlie that you don't want a Christmas tree," Dusty offered as an opening for another argument.

She ignored him and took her old coat off its hook beside the back door. "See you all later," she said.

When the door closed behind her, she grinned with relief. "Come on, Emily, hurry. Louise might be in the park already."

Louise Stone lived on the opposite side of the small park two blocks away, so the three girls always chose the playground as a meeting place.

"How much food did you bring?" Molly asked, eyeing the grocery bag Emily carried.

"Plenty," Emily answered. "I fixed lunch myself. My mother is crabby again, because Nancy's cold is worse, and Dad has to work at the hotel, so he won't be home for dinner. She hates that hotel, and she hates the bad weather."

"She still misses Hawaii," Molly said with a pang. Even though Emily and her family had lived in Seattle for three years, she knew they never got over being homesick.

"But when we were there, she hated the heat and the bugs and Dad working in a restaurant," Emily said, sighing.

They found Louise on a swing, pushing herself idly with her good leg. "Is that our lunch? I hope you two can work up a big appetite, because Mother sent along about a thousand chocolate cookies." She held up a bulging sack. "Let's get started. The wind feels colder every minute."

On the way to the beach, Molly described her encounters with Paul Gardner at the movies and at church. The others were properly impressed, especially with her description of Mrs. Gardner's red coat.

Emily entertained them with delicious hints about their Christmas presents. She was a more imaginative gift-giver than anyone else Molly knew — and a bigger tease.

Louise shared the satisfying news that she had seen ugly Daryl Arthur, the school bully, smoking a cigarette behind the junior high school gym.

"Did he get caught?" Molly asked, full of hope.

"What brand was he smoking?" asked Emily, who liked to hear every detail.

"I don't know what brand," Louise said, "but he sicked up in the place where the janitor parks his truck."

They reached the railroad tracks in ten minutes, crossed over, scrambled through a narrow strip of winter-ravaged brush, and stepped out on the wet, gray sand. Half a dozen other people poked along the water's edge, but none of them seemed interested in collecting anything.

The girls left their lunch sacks beside a pile of driftwood and went off in different directions to search for shells. Gulls swooped above them in the cold salty air, shrieking with excitement. Out on the water, a ferry wallowed clumsily toward a distant island. A heavy freighter ploughed northward, carrying unimaginable treasures to places that were only names on a map to Molly.

She walked north, out of sight of the cluster of small, sagging old beach cottages across the railroad tracks from the water. Along the way, she picked up three clamshells, all close to the same size. She found a fourth perfect shell in a tangle of seaweed and bent her head to examine it. The inner lining glowed with a sort of light, as if it had been touched with magic. Molly decided to keep it for herself instead of using it for the project, and slipped it into her skirt pocket.

After she turned back, when Emily and Louise were

once again in sight, she thought she saw Uncle Charlie crossing the tracks. No, she must be mistaken, she told herself.

But then she heard his shout. "Molly! Girls! Come here!"

Molly and Emily ran toward him, and Louise struggled along as best she could, her red curls blowing around her face.

"What is it?" Molly called out. "What's wrong?"

A dozen frightening ideas crowded her mind. Something was wrong with her parents, with Dusty, with the house. Someone had died — one of the Donnelly aunts? Mama's sister?

She grabbed Uncle Charlie's arm when she reached him. He put out his free hand to pat Emily's shoulder. "Louise, you all right?" he asked, as the girl struggled toward him.

"What's wrong?" Molly asked again.

"The Japanese bombed Pearl Harbor," Uncle Charlie said. "We're at war."

"Where's Pearl Harbor?" Molly had never heard of it.

"That's where my auntie lives!" Emily screamed. "She's dead, isn't she? Auntie's dead!"

"Pearl Harbor's in Hawaii, Molly," Uncle Charlie said. "Come on, girls. I've got the car on the other side of the tracks, so I'll drive everybody home."

Later, Molly would remember that they had left their lunch behind. But a forgotten lunch would never be important again.

2

Evening, December 7, 1941

We listened to war news on the radio until dark,
when the station went off the air so that Japanese
planes can't follow the signal to Seattle and bomb us.
It's hard for us to believe this is really happening.
There is a blackout, so I'm writing this under my
covers by flashlight.

That night Molly did not sleep well. Several times she
heard aircraft overhead, and she rushed to her window to
raise the shade and watch searchlights crossing and recross-
ing the sky, fingering clouds, finally locating the planes and
illuminating their bellies.

Kneeling at her window, fascinated and terrified, Molly
waited for bombs to fall. But nothing happened. The planes
were American.

And then, strangely, in the middle of the night, Molly
heard a piercing wail from next door. Mrs. Tanaka's voice

rose and fell for several seconds and then died away. Molly pulled her blankets over her head.

She woke to her mother's voice at the door, cautioning her.

"Don't turn on your light," Mama said. "The blackout lasts until eight o'clock."

Molly groaned and rolled out of bed. Her toes curled up in protest when they touched the cold floor.

Her mother hurried down the hall to wake Dusty, who whined and finally wept, protesting the darkness, the morning, and the idea of school.

"I can't go to school," he cried. "The Japs are coming! Where will I hide?"

"Don't say Japs," Mama said automatically. "Mrs. Barrows called and said she heard on the radio that the schools will be open, so Tom and Tim are going. She said it's their duty as Americans."

"If the Ts are going, then I'll go too," Dusty said. "I'm just as brave as they are, and lots more than Nancy Tanaka. Is she going to school? She better not try walking with us!"

Nancy, Emily's sister, was eight years old too, but Dusty and the Ts never walked to school with her — not that she wanted them tagging along, Molly suspected.

"I wouldn't be surprised if the Tanaka girls stayed home," Mama said as she came back down the hall, her slippers flapping on the thin carpet. She stuck her head in Molly's door. "You getting dressed?"

Molly cleared her throat and said, "As soon as I finish in the bathroom."

Mrs. Donnelly darted in the door. "You caught cold out on the beach, didn't you? Come downstairs and let me have a look at you. We've got light in the kitchen."

Molly followed her down, groping along the stairway. The door that separated the kitchen from the dining room was shut for the first time in her memory.

"Scoot through quickly," Mama said. "Ready? Follow me."

They rushed headlong into the bright kitchen, and Mama slammed the door behind them.

"See what your dad did last night?" Mama said, pointing to the window over the sink and the glass panel in the door. Each window had been fitted with a neatly cut piece of cardboard. "No light can get out, so I can see to cook breakfast in the mornings. We could spend the evenings in here, too."

"We have to?" Molly croaked.

"Open your mouth and let me see your tonsils," her mother commanded. She pulled Molly until she stood in the center of the room, under the light. Obediently, Molly opened her mouth.

"No, it's not your tonsils, but your throat is red and raw. Sit down and I'll get the roof tar."

"Roof tar" was what Uncle Charlie called the thick, black syrup that Molly's mother forced on everyone who caught a cold.

"No, Mama, please," Molly begged.

But her mother came back from the pantry with the dreaded bottle and grabbed up a spoon from the counter as she passed it.

"I'll give you two spoonsful, just in case."

Molly gagged down the syrup and made a face.

"And you'll stay home from school," her mother added.

"I can't!" Molly cried. "Everybody will think I'm too scared to go."

"You're not leaving the house with that red throat," Mama said. "I'll tell Emily when she stops by for you. If she does."

"Dad and Uncle Charlie went to work?" Molly asked. She sipped her juice, but it tasted like roof tar.

"They went early. They thought it would be a good idea."

Dusty trailed into the room, rubbing his fists in his eyes.

"Shut the door!" Mrs. Donnelly cried. She explained about the kitchen light again, but Molly could see that Dusty wasn't listening.

"Where's my hotcakes?" he demanded.

"We're having cold cereal . . . oh, for heaven's sake, Dusty. Get that look off your face and sit down to eat."

"You're sure the Ts are going to school?"

"I'm sure. But Molly's staying home because she's sick." Mama poured milk over Dusty's cold cereal and ignored his complaints.

As usual, he dawdled and whined over his breakfast, and afterward lost, then found, then lost again his socks, his jacket, and finally his lunch.

"How could you lose it on the way to the door?" Mrs. Donnelly yelled.

She found the lunch immediately, wedged between Uncle Charlie's chair and the wall, and thrust it at Dusty.

"Do you want me to walk down to the Barrows's with you?" she asked.

"In your old bathrobe?" Dusty shouted. "And have everybody think I can't cross the street by myself?"

He stormed out, leaving the back door open and light streaming out into the wet dawn.

Mrs. Donnelly leaped for the door and slammed it shut. Then, suddenly, without any warning, she burst into tears.

"What if something happens to him?" she cried.

"Call him back," Molly said. Was her mother worried about Dusty being injured in an air raid, or was something else wrong?

"No, we can't panic over everything," Mrs. Donnelly said. "Your father said you children ought to go to school, that we should do all the things we ordinarily do. If everybody panics, then things can only get worse."

"Then let me go to school, too," Molly said.

"And risk your getting tonsillitis again?" her mother asked. "No. Finish your breakfast and I'll make up a bed for you on the couch."

The time came and passed for Emily to stop by the house for Molly on her way to school. At eight o'clock, Mrs. Donnelly took the cardboard down from the kitchen windows, and when Molly looked out, she saw that the Tanakas' car was in the driveway. Apparently Mr. Tanaka had not gone to work at the hotel owned by his cousin. But the house looked deserted.

"I've got to start the washing," her mother said. "Just let me get the whites soaking, and then I'll fix a bed for you downstairs."

Molly's throat did not hurt until she was alone in the living room, tucked up in a bundle of quilts and pillows. Bored and lonely, she watched out the windows, but nothing was happening in the street.

The Tanakas must be worried, Molly thought. Dad had said that it might take a while before they learned if their relatives in Pearl Harbor were all right.

The Donnellys were concerned about Maureen, Charlie's daughter, who was an army nurse stationed in the Philippine Islands, also under attack by the Japanese. But Uncle Charlie was sure the nurses would be evacuated right away if things looked bad, if the enemy got too close.

A car pulled up in front of the Tanakas'. Molly propped herself on one elbow to watch two strange men hurry up to the Tanakas' door. She waited, curious, and then saw one of the men come back out, carrying the Tanakas' radio and what looked like their camera.

Something was wrong. Molly jumped up from the couch and ran through the house to the basement stairs. "Mama!" she cried hoarsely. "Two men are taking things away from the Tanakas' house!"

Her mother ran up the stairs, stumbling once and nearly falling to her knees. "What are you talking about?"

"Men, two of them, at the Tanakas'."

They couldn't see the Tanakas' front yard from the kitchen, so they ran to the living room. Mrs. Donnelly frightened Molly by opening the front door and stepping out to the porch. Hadn't she seen what Molly had seen through the window over the couch? The man who stole the Tanakas' big radio from the living room was now carrying out the small radio from Emily's room. They were burglars and probably dangerous.

"Mama, shut the door," Molly called out.

"It's a free country and I'll watch if I want to," Mrs. Donnelly said angrily. She leaned on the porch railing and cupped her hands around her mouth. "Hey, you two! I see what you're doing!"

The man with Emily's radio threw it into the trunk of the car, then marched back up the walk. If he heard Mrs. Donnelly, he pretended that he didn't.

Cold air blew in through the open door. Molly pulled a quilt from the couch and wrapped it around her shoulders, then went to stand behind her mother.

Mr. Tanaka came out, wearing a suit and a hat. The two men walked beside him, close beside him, as if they were afraid he would run away from them. They put him into the back seat of the car, climbed into the front, and drove away.

Across the street and down the block, Mrs. Barrows must have seen the whole thing, for Molly heard her shout, "Serves him right. All those Japs are spies."

Mrs. Donnelly pushed Molly inside and slammed the door. "Spies, my foot!" Mama exclaimed. "What on earth is going on? Burglars wouldn't take away Mr. Tanaka. I'm going next door and find out what's happening."

"I'll come," Molly said.

"You stay on the couch," her mother said. "I don't have the time or patience for nursing you through another bout of tonsil troubles." She hurried out the back door and across the lawns to the Tanakas' back door.

Molly waited for as long as she could stand it, then finally pulled her old coat on over her pajamas and followed her mother next door.

The Tanakas' kitchen was smaller than the Donnellys', and it was crowded with the two women, Emily, Nancy, and Molly. No one was sitting, so Molly stood too.

"What happened?" she asked fearfully.

"They took Mr. Tanaka away to question him," her mother said. "They didn't say why or for how long. It has something to do with his being born in Japan."

"He doesn't remember Japan!" Mrs. Tanaka cried, her voice shrill. "His parents took him to Hawaii when he was only a baby. He's never been back to Japan. He doesn't write letters to anybody there, only to relatives in Hawaii. We are Americans, just like you. Why did those FBI men do this to us?"

Emily and Nancy were silent, frozen, their dark eyes solemn.

"Are you all right?" Molly asked Emily.

Emily nodded. "How come you didn't go to school?"

"I've got a cold."

Molly's mother interrupted her. "Mrs. Tanaka, I think you should call your husband's cousin at the hotel. Maybe he knows something."

"I tried, but no one answers the phone," Mrs. Tanaka said.

"Then you should go there and see what you can find out," Mrs. Donnelly said. "Can somebody take you? I don't know how to drive, and I know you can't either, but surely there's somebody who'll help you."

"I'll find someone," Mrs. Tanaka said.

"Leave the girls with me," Mrs. Donnelly said.

"I don't want to be separated from them," Mrs. Tanaka said. "Not today."

"Will you let me know what you find out?" Mrs. Donnelly asked.

Mrs. Tanaka hesitated, then nodded.

"Call me, Emily," Molly whispered. "As soon as you find out what happened to your dad, call. This is probably some kind of mistake."

"Go home," Emily's sister said suddenly. Her face was screwed tight with anger. "You go home, Molly."

"Nancy!" Emily cried.

"Go home!" Nancy shouted, running at Molly, her fists doubled up. "Go home, you *Jap*!"

"Nancy, stop it!" her mother cried, grabbing Nancy's arm.

Molly backed close to the wall, shocked.

"I'll wait to hear from you," her mother told Mrs. Tanaka. She opened the door and beckoned to Molly to follow her.

Molly did not say a word until they reached their own kitchen. "I can't believe Nancy called me a Jap," she said.

"She probably thinks it's a word like 'fathead' or 'fool.' Goodness knows she's heard it enough times around this neighborhood, thanks to Mrs. Barrows and her twins."

And Dusty, Molly added to herself.

She went back to bed on the couch, and after a long time, she saw another car stop in front of the Tanakas'. A young Japanese man jumped out and ran up the walk. Moments later, Mrs. Tanaka and the girls came out of the house. Molly waved and she was certain that Emily saw her, but Emily didn't wave back. The car pulled away from the curb, turned the corner, and was gone.

Molly was still lying on the couch when Dusty came home, full of school gossip. He carried a paper American flag he had made in class, and a large blue poster with a big red *V* for victory pasted on it, along with three dots and a dash.

"What does that mean?" Molly asked, pointing to the dots and dash.

"That's Morse code for the letter *V*," Dusty told her, insufferable with pride at knowing something that Molly didn't. "Dit-dit-dit-dah. And we learned about air raid sirens and dive-bombers and all that stuff. And guess what? There are three great big balloon things in the air over the vacant lot next to Peterson's gas station. They look like blimps, but they're called barrage balloons. And there are more of them down toward town. They'll keep Jap dive-bombers away from us. And I learned another verse to 'The Star-Spangled Banner,' too."

"So what?" Molly grumbled, sinking back into what she now thought of as her bed of suffering and pain.

Dad and Uncle Charlie came home later than usual because they had to drive without headlights. Mama told them about the Tanakas as soon as they took off their coats.

"What are you talking about?" Dad asked, astonished.

"Joe, two men came and took Mr. Tanaka away," Mama explained again. "Mrs. Tanaka and the girls left to see if they can find out what's going on. They're probably at the hotel."

"Have you called there to see what she says?" Uncle Charlie asked.

"No one answers," Mama said.

"There are people who want all Japanese moved into detention camps to keep them from blowing up the factories," Dad said.

Molly tried to imagine Mr. Tanaka blowing up a factory and failed.

"Of course, there are people who want everybody with German or Italian names locked up, too," Uncle Charlie said.

"But that's practically half of all the people we know," Mrs. Donnelly cried. "That's stupid!"

"Don't tell me, Jenny, tell Dinah Barrows," Uncle Charlie said. "It's people like her who like the idea. They always seem to have a cup of gasoline to toss into a fire."

Molly went to bed after dinner, to lie awake and listen for someone arriving home next door. But no one came.

After a while, Uncle Charlie knocked on her door and stepped inside.

"Are you here in the dark, or am I talking to myself?" he asked.

"I'm here," Molly answered. "Be careful not to fall over my shoes."

He sat on the chair beside her desk. "So what do you think of all this, Margaret Mary Donnelly?"

23

"I hate thinking about it," Molly said. "I wish it was still last week."

"But it's not," Uncle Charlie said. "It's an age and an age since last week, and we're stuck with it."

"A lot of people are dead," Molly said. "I heard that on the news."

"Yes."

"I guess you saw lots of people die in the big war when you were a soldier, didn't you, Charlie?" Molly asked.

"That's a sad truth," he said after a long pause.

"I guess you're scared for Maureen, aren't you?"

Charlie cleared his throat. "The army will evacuate the nurses to a safe place," he said.

He leaned forward and Molly heard something fall on her bed, near her face. "That's the rosary Maureen carried when she was confirmed," he said. "I thought maybe you'd pray for her, if you don't have enough to do while you're lying there thinking up grand excuses to keep you out of school until you're thirty."

Molly clutched the rosary beads and blinked to keep from crying. "I've got enough excuses to last longer than that, Charlie Donnelly. But I'm going back to school tomorrow anyway, to make a liar out of you."

"Oh, God, listen to her," Charlie moaned. "She's all sass and shameful disrespect. Is that how You're rewarding me for never missing confession once in fifty years, and me with my white hair and bad back?"

"You're only forty-five years old, Charlie," Molly said, laughing now. "And you've missed confession lots of times."

Charlie got to his feet and walked to the door. "I can't keep up with you, girl. You're too smart for me. Sleep well and dream about what I'm giving you for Christmas."

But Christmas seemed an impossibly distant holiday. Molly fell asleep listening to the cold wind feeling its way under the eaves outside her window.

✢ 3

Evening, December 9, 1941

I hate blackouts. The whole world is dark, and cold,
and full of changes. Everyone in my class but me
forgot our seashell projects. Nobody talks about
Christmas. Paul Gardner says that yesterday was his
cousin's birthday and nobody remembered to give
him his gifts.

On Tuesday, Molly walked part of the way to school with
Dusty and the Ts. The boys didn't appreciate her company,
and let her know in every rude way they could invent.

"Don't think I won't tell Mama how you act," Molly said,
after Dusty yelled that she walked like a duck.

"Go ahead," Dusty retaliated. "She won't believe anything you say."

Molly fell back and let the boys race ahead of her. This
was her last year in grade school. Next year she would have
her eighth grade classes in the junior high, which was really
just a wing on the high school with separate entrances,

although the students always spoke of it as if it were a building all to itself. Then Molly would no longer even walk the same route as her brother and the Ts, and that was a thought worth treasuring.

She and Emily would walk east, passing beside a long row of poplars and the biggest cherry tree in the neighborhood.

If Emily moved back to the house.

Molly found Louise combing her hair in the girls' first-floor lavatory.

"Where's Emily?" Louise asked. "Isn't she coming today, either?"

"Some men from the FBI took her father away yesterday. We think she and Nancy and their mother went to the hotel where he worked, to see if they could find out what was going on, but they didn't come back, so we still don't know anything."

"None of the Japanese kids came to school yesterday," Louise said. "I haven't seen any this morning, either. Mother says it's probably safer for them. Some of the boys say awful things out on the playground."

"What awful things?" Molly asked.

"Oh, stuff about beating up the Japs."

Molly pulled off her red knit cap and stared at herself in the mirror. Her face was pale, her eyes ringed with shadows. "Everybody's crazy. Dad and Uncle Charlie said some people want to lock up everybody with German or Italian names because they might be spies."

"You mean like my Grandma Schiller? She was born in Seattle! She doesn't even know how to speak German. And she's nearly blind. How could she be a spy?"

"How could Emily's father be a spy?" Molly asked. "He has such bad rheumatism that he walks with a cane half the time."

"You're right," Louise said. "Everybody's crazy."

When they reached class, Daryl Arthur asked Molly where her Jap friend was. She ignored him until he poked her hard with his pencil.

"Where is she?" he demanded. "Is she helping her family blow up factories?"

The room was slowly filling with students, and the nearest ones sucked in their breath.

Molly turned on Daryl in a fury. "She's from Hawaii, not Japan, stupid! From Hawaii! That means she's an American. Maybe her aunt was killed on Sunday at Pearl Harbor. How would you like it if your aunt was killed?"

"I'd be glad if she was a Jap," Daryl said, smirking.

"Hey!" Louise cried. "You just shut up, Daryl Arthur, or I'll tell Molly how the boys found you bawling in the art supply cupboard yesterday during the air raid drill."

The other kids laughed, and Daryl, sensing the mood in the room, took his seat near the wall and glared at the girls.

Molly knew he'd try to get even with her, sooner or later. He was the meanest boy she'd ever known.

When Molly got home that afternoon, nursing the bruise Daryl had made on her arm during recess, she found her mother helping Mrs. Tanaka and an elderly Japanese man load boxes and bags into the Tanakas' car. She said hello to Mrs. Tanaka, but the woman didn't answer.

Rebuffed, Molly followed her mother into the kitchen, where Emily and Nancy were transferring things from drawers to a cardboard box on the floor.

When Grandma Donnelly had been alive, this room always smelled of fresh-baked bread and strong coffee. Now, in spite of her bad cold, Molly could smell the ghosts of fish and onions and something she couldn't define.

Emily had told her once, when she first moved in, that white people smelled bad because they drank milk. Molly had thought that Emily was terribly rude, but she restrained herself from saying that the Tanaka family always smelled slightly of fish. Remembering it embarrassed Molly now. She felt as if she were betraying her friend somehow, thinking of something so unpleasant at a time like this. Perhaps she remembered it because Mrs. Tanaka had ignored her when she arrived, and Nancy was frankly glaring at her — as if any of this was her fault!

"How come you're moving out?" she asked Emily.

"Dad and his cousin have been arrested, so the rest of the family will live together until we know what's going to happen to us." Emily wrapped measuring spoons in a napkin and placed it carefully in the box. She seemed uneasy and avoided looking up. "You sound like you have an awful cold, Molly."

"I'm fine," Molly said. She glanced at her mother, who was pulling pans out of a cupboard. "I'm lots better."

There seemed to be nothing left to say, nothing that was safe. Molly longed to ask Emily if she was afraid, if she was going to start a new school, if she knew yet whether her aunt had been killed. But the girls who had spent so many hours together for three years were left with only the polite exchanges that strangers make.

"Maybe you could call me from the hotel," Molly asked. "I could call you, if I knew the number."

"We can't use the telephone," Nancy cried suddenly, red with rage. "We can't use the telephone because people might be listening to us and maybe they'll take us away, too."

Nancy ran out to the porch, leaving Emily blinking and shrugging helplessly. But before Emily left that day, she pressed into Molly's hand a scrap of paper with a phone number written on it.

"If anybody but me answers," she whispered, "hang up. If I can't talk to you, I'll write you. If I can."

It didn't take long for the Tanakas to pack up their things, for all the furniture in the house belonged to the Donnellys. When the last of the clothes and books were loaded into the car, Molly had a moment with Emily on the porch.

"Maybe you'll be back pretty soon," Molly whispered.

"Sure," Emily said. "We'll go to the beach and have our picnic."

"No, I meant maybe you'll move back into the house."

"Get in the car," Emily's mother told her. She yanked Emily's arm, pulling her away from Molly.

Emily scrambled into the back seat, wedging herself between cardboard boxes and heaps of sheets and towels. She waved once and then looked away. Mrs. Tanaka didn't respond to Mrs. Donnelly's goodbyes.

"Nancy and her mother act as if this was our fault," Molly said as they watched the car turn the corner. "Mrs. Tanaka didn't even thank you for helping her."

"She's probably terrified," Mrs. Donnelly said. "I know I would be. Who knows what will happen to them?"

Molly called the phone number many times that evening, but no one answered.

Molly's father arrived home without Uncle Charlie that evening. He came as close as he ever did to smiling when Molly asked what had happened to her uncle.

"He'll be along pretty soon," Mr. Donnelly said. "He's got a surprise."

"But you know what it is, don't you?" Molly asked.

"Maybe I do and maybe I don't," her father said. He set his lunch box down on the counter and reached for the coffeepot that Molly's mother kept on the back of the stove. "Cold out tonight."

"What's the surprise?" Dusty demanded. "I want to know."

Mrs. Donnelly took a mug from the cupboard and poured her husband's coffee for him. "I could do with a surprise, a nice one."

"You'll like it, that's all I'm going to say," Mr. Donnelly told them.

In the street, someone honked a horn over and over.

Molly and Dusty ran toward the living room, and Mrs. Donnelly called after them, "Don't turn on the lights!"

They ran out on the porch and saw, in the dark, the outline of a truck they didn't recognize.

"Who's there?" Dusty shouted.

"It's Santa Claus, come to see how much mischief you've made this last year!"

"Uncle Charlie!" Dusty shouted. "Whose truck is that? Why didn't you come home with Dad? What's the surprise?"

Uncle Charlie and another man busied themselves at the back of the truck. Finally Uncle Charlie said, "Thanks, Don. See you tomorrow."

He walked toward the porch, dragging something behind him.

"It's a Christmas tree," Molly said. "Everybody forgot about the tree on Sunday."

"You said I could go with you to Cheap Jack's for the tree!" Dusty whined. "Why didn't you come home for me first?"

Uncle Charlie let the tree drop on the front walk. "I didn't go to Cheap Jack's. This is a special tree. I got it at that fancy place — what's it called? Christmas Spirit?"

Molly hugged herself. Christmas Spirit was the shop that opened only once a year behind the garden store, selling rare and special trees and decorations so beautiful that people crowded outside the windows to stare at the displays. But everything the shop sold was too expensive for the Donnellys. It was a place they went to daydream.

"Is it sprayed white?" Molly asked. "I can't see. Is it? Is it?"

"Your mother would kill me if I brought home a white tree," Uncle Charlie said as he joined them on the porch. "No, ma'am, it's not white."

Molly couldn't wait any longer. She jumped off the porch and knelt beside the tree, touching it gingerly, feeling the prick of long needles.

"You got a long-needle pine," she said. "It's what Mama always wanted."

"And that's not all," Charlie said. "What's a long-needle pine without special decorations?"

Molly saw then that he carried a shopping bag in one hand.

"From Christmas Spirit?" Molly squealed.

"I can't believe you wasted your money this way," Molly's mother said from the doorway. But Molly could hear the smile in her voice.

"Moira and Maureen always wanted a tree from Christmas Spirit," Uncle Charlie said. He was silent for a moment. "I never thought I could afford anything that fancy. So, in a way, this tree's for my own dears, both of them, but the rest of us get to enjoy it, too."

"Bring it inside," Mrs. Donnelly said. "I'm starting to feel as if Christmas is really coming again."

"Did you get a star for the top, Uncle Charlie?" Molly asked, her eyes on the shopping bag. "Did you get tinsel? Did you get any of those balls with the Christmas fairies inside?"

"Oh, my God, listen to Princess Margaret Mary," Uncle Charlie said. "I do my best for her, but You aren't satisfied, are You? Will You quit telling her all the ways she can spend my money? This feels more like Lent than Christmas."

Molly tried once more that evening to call Emily at the hotel, to ask her if she had heard anything about her father. But there was no answer.

No answer.

By candlelight that night, the Donnellys decorated their tree. Molly glued a bit of yarn to the perfect shell she had found on the beach and hung it on a high branch, thinking of Emily.

I'll give it to her when she comes back, she thought.

🐝 4

December 1941

This is the first time I've written in my new journal. Uncle Charlie gave it to me for Christmas. It's made of leather and has my name printed on it in gold letters. Uncle Charlie said it's time I stopped keeping a child's diary and began writing essays about life. I'm not sure I know how to write any kind of essay. He told me it's like writing a philosophical letter to yourself. Later, he whispered that Dusty isn't likely to be interested in philosophical observations, especially if I use big words.

Christmas was strange that year. By the time Molly's father had cut cardboard to fit all the windows in the house and hung blankets over the doors that led outside to serve as barriers against any stray beam of light, the blackout was lifted, at least in the early evening hours. But the family only decorated the inside of the house and left the outside bare and dark. The neighborhood seemed sad.

On Christmas Eve, the house filled with relatives who brought gifts and food. Molly's father and uncle had two sisters, younger than Charlie, but older than Joe. Aunt Elizabeth was a widow with two daughters, both older than Molly. Sharon, at fifteen, looked like most of the Donnellys, with black hair and blue eyes. But Monica, seventeen, had blond hair, and she was as beautiful as the tiny glass fairies imprisoned inside the transparent balls that decorated the Christmas tree. Molly thought that Monica could be a movie star, but Monica had a "vocation," meaning that she wanted to be a nun. Aunt Elizabeth was terribly proud of Monica's vocation, but Molly's mother had told Molly once that Monica was the next thing to simple-minded.

Aunt Bridget, married to fat, laughing Francis O'Brien, had a sixteen-year-old son, Frank Junior, and a fourteen-year-old daughter, Mary Lou, both redheads like Uncle Francis.

Aunt Bridget was different from Aunt Elizabeth, and not only because she drank as much as her brothers and laughed as much as Charlie. When she walked in the house, she said, "What a beautiful tree! The house smells wonderful. Look at you, Molly — you're the prettiest thing."

Aunt Elizabeth, on the other hand, said, "How can you people afford a tree like this in such hard times? Molly, hang up my coat and try to do something about your slip. It shows in back."

Mrs. Donnelly had a sister, Eva, married to John Parsons. Their daughter, Darlene, was fourteen. Their son, Eddie, was ten. Both children had reddish brown hair like their mother, Mrs. Donnelly, and Dusty. All of them had freckles. Aunt Eva was thin and moody, and spent most of Christmas Eve complaining about her neighbors who openly bragged about hoarding coffee and sugar against the time when they would be in short supply.

"Have another hot cider," Uncle Charlie told her, passing her the tray he had just carried in from the kitchen. He winked at Molly. "This is Christmas Eve. We're the luckiest people alive, to have each other and Jenny's good spiced cider, all at the same time."

Aunt Eva took the cider but she didn't smile.

Darlene followed Molly out to the kitchen. "Isn't there a Japanese family living next door?"

Molly refilled a bowl with Christmas cookies. "There was, but they moved away."

"My Japanese friend played the violin next to me in our school orchestra," Darlene said. "She still comes to school, but she doesn't play anymore. Not even for the Christmas concert."

"Maybe she'll come back to the orchestra," Molly said.

Darlene shook her head. "I don't think so. Everything's changed. What about Maureen? Have you heard anything?"

"Not yet," Molly said. "Carry in that plate of fudge for me, will you?"

Darlene followed her back to the living room, her taffeta skirt whispering as she walked. Molly knew her cousin

37

meant well, asking about Maureen, but she didn't like to be questioned. Sometimes people asked right out if Maureen was dead.

Their neighbor, Mrs. Dinah Barrows, had told Molly's mother two days before Christmas, in Molly's hearing, that she had heard the army nurses had been captured and raped by the Japanese soldiers. As soon as Mrs. Barrows had gone home, Molly asked her mother what "raped" meant. Her mother, white and near tears, told her to never mind, she wasn't old enough to know yet. So Molly looked up the word "rape" in the unabridged dictionary. It meant "carnal knowledge." Molly looked up "carnal," but didn't understand what she read and finally gave up. But she had added to her prayers at night that no carnal knowledge would happen to Maureen.

Eddie and Dusty sat together on the steps leading upstairs from the dining room, talking about comic books and gobbling Christmas cookies. Sharon and Mary Lou primped in the mirror that hung over the buffet. Frank Junior talked about airplanes with the men.

And Monica, pretty Monica who had a vocation, sat in the small music room off the living room, quietly playing Christmas carols on the piano. The lamplight fell on her pale hair, and Molly could have cried because Monica was so beautiful, exactly like an angel. Which was, of course, better than looking like a Christmas fairy, although Molly wasn't sure why. It might have been the difference in wings. Angel wings were feathered, but fairies seemed to have wings made of the same stuff as butterfly wings. Molly decided that the distinction might be worth recording in her journal.

Late in the evening the guests began leaving, taking with them the Christmas gifts they would open the next morning. Dusty, tired and cranky, was sent to bed complaining bitterly that they had not had their usual wooden crate of Japanese oranges that Christmas Eve.

"Merry Christmas," Molly called to him as he staggered up the stairs. "Just think, Santa Claus will be here in a few hours."

"I don't believe in Santa Claus," Dusty cried. "I never did. Only you are dumb enough to believe in him, Molly."

"Merry Christmas," Uncle Charlie whispered in Molly's ear. "You and I believe in Santa, don't we?"

"You bet," Molly said. "We believe in everything nice."

"Are you going to midnight mass with me?" Uncle Charlie asked.

"Don't I always go?" Molly asked. Midnight mass was the perfect finish to Christmas Eve, she thought.

It began at eleven-thirty, but if they wanted good seats, they had to leave early. Uncle Charlie and Molly left the house at ten forty-five. The night sky was strewn with stars and smelled of fir trees and wood smoke. They walked only a block or two alone, and then, by twos and threes, other people joined them, until they arrived at the church with a small crowd. For once, no one mentioned the war.

The church was fragrant with everything wonderful — evergreens and candles and incense and the cologne the ladies wore. Even the harsher smells — damp wool and mothballs — seemed somehow festive.

Molly waited while Uncle Charlie lit the candle for Aunt Moira, and then sat with him in a pew where she could see everything.

How could anything go wrong in a world that had a midnight mass in it, she wondered.

But on the way home, Mr. and Mrs. Polaski walked with them and wanted to talk about the war in the Philippines. Their daughter Mary, who was Maureen's best friend, was also an army nurse stationed there. When Molly heard Mrs. Polaski sob, she ran ahead in the dark, not caring if she stumbled or not.

She was ashamed, but she could not bear the pain in their voices as they spoke of their daughters and what might be happening to them. Christmas was spoiled for Molly.

In the morning, after she opened her gifts, she put away the blouse and beads Maureen had sent her. She would wear them when Maureen came home and not before.

A few days later, Molly received a late Christmas card from Emily. Her friend had written nothing inside but her name. The envelope bore no return address. Molly had sent a card and a gift to the hotel before Christmas, and she was puzzled that Emily did not mention receiving either of them.

Molly showed the card to her mother. "Why didn't she write something?"

"Maybe because she was afraid her mother would find out," Mrs. Donnelly said. "Probably I shouldn't tell you this, but Mrs. Tanaka thought that maybe her husband was taken away because he lived next door to Charlie."

"What's wrong with Uncle Charlie?" Molly asked, astonished.

"It's not what's wrong with him. It's what he does."

"He works for the Boeing company, like Dad, like Mr. Barrows. We know lots of people who work there."

"Uncle Charlie does something special for them," Mama said. "Something very secret."

"Like what?" Molly asked.

Mama shrugged uncomfortably. "He's never even told your father. But for the last year, after they enter the gate, he goes to a different building with extra guards around it. That's all I know. Last summer I made the mistake of telling that to Mrs. Tanaka. It was a sort of joke. Charlie and his secret project. You know what a clown he is. Who would think he could keep any kind of secret?" She sighed and pressed her fingers to her lips. "I shouldn't have said anything to her. I'm sure it didn't have one thing to do with Mr. Tanaka's arrest. They were arresting all the men born in Japan. But . . . well, she was upset that day, and she's always been high-strung."

"But what has that got to do with Emily not phoning or writing to me?" Molly asked.

"Maybe her mother thinks that people might get the idea they were spying on Charlie and the other men around here who work for the war factories. People have some strange ideas at times like this. Be patient. You'll hear from Emily pretty soon, when people aren't so nervous."

February 1942

Nothing is the same as it was a year ago. Seattle is full of soldiers and sailors. There are convoys of ships in the Sound, and lines of army trucks carrying men on the highway I cross on my way to school. I've seen trainloads of tanks and guns pass the place on the beach where Emily and Louise and I used to play. There are barrage balloons everywhere, and anti-aircraft guns in vacant lots.

Finally Molly received a letter from Emily, in February, when the snowdrops and first yellow primroses were blooming in the flowerbeds.

"You are my best friend in Seattle," Emily wrote. "The best times I had after I left Hawaii were with you. I don't know what will happen to us, but before we leave, I will try to get back once to see you. Watch for me."

By that time, everyone had learned from newspapers and the radio that all American Japanese were to be sent away and locked up in internment camps. Molly wept over the letter and kept it with her journal, under her mattress.

I'll watch for you, Emily, she thought. Every day.

The next Sunday afternoon, when the sky was pale blue and streaked with thin white clouds and the earth smelled like spring, Molly and her family went to the hotel where Mrs. Tanaka and the girls were staying. They brought with them cookies and candy, and an armload of pussy willows and forsythia. Molly's mother wanted to assure the Tanakas that they would keep Grandma Donnelly's house for them, instead of renting it to another family.

The front door of the shabby little hotel was locked. No one came when Mr. Donnelly knocked and called out, but Molly saw an unfamiliar face at a second-floor window. An unsmiling face.

They carried their offerings of friendship away, and Mrs. Donnelly cried for a long time.

"I don't blame them for not coming to the door," she said. "They must be afraid of us now, of what we can do to them, of what we *are* doing."

Molly waited, hoping to see Emily one more time before the evacuation of the Japanese began. Once, on a misty Saturday morning, she walked to the beach alone, and as she crossed the railroad tracks, she thought she saw Emily far down the beach, sitting in one of their favorite spots.

"Emily!" she shouted. "Emily!"

But a strange, dark-haired girl jumped to her feet, one of the new girls in school, someone Molly didn't know.

Molly shook her head angrily and turned away, not willing to be friends with an outsider.

A line of ships in camouflage paint sailed north, engines throbbing, toward the Strait that connected Puget Sound to the ocean — and the war in the Pacific.

Later that spring, Molly's father said, "This war might last a long time and the Tanakas won't be back until the end of it. No matter how hard it is, we'd better face up to the way things are now. So many people need housing, and I think we need to consider renting Grandma's house again."

"Joe," Molly's mother cried. "How can you say that? What would the Tanakas think if they came back and found somebody else there?"

"Joe's right," Uncle Charlie said. "It's cruel, the way some families are living. We've got a nice house sitting empty next door. Let's do the right thing, Jenny."

"No, please," Molly said, certain that if someone else lived in the house and Emily heard about it, she would never forgive the Donnellys.

"Joe, Charlie — give me time to think about it," her mother said, her fingers pressing her temples. "I just can't do it right now."

But Molly knew that another change was taking place. Emily had been gone for many weeks. Life was happening without her.

⚡5

July 1942

I don't know what is wrong with this family.
Sometimes all we do is fight. Maybe the war is the
cause of it. Things that should be funny drive us
crazy, like the imitation leather shoes Mama bought
because she couldn't find real leather ones that fit.
The tops came off the soles while she waited for the
bus in the rain. She came home and yelled at me!

She and Louise's mother stand in line for hours
for meat, and then can only get pork sausage or a
few slices of bacon. The Ts brag that their mother
buys meat on the black market, so they have steak
and roast beef.

I wonder what Emily eats. She hates sausage.

"Molly's in love, Molly's in love," Dusty chanted outside the
bathroom door.

Molly slammed her hairbrush down in the edge of the
basin. I ought to knock his silly block off, she thought. And

the Ts are out there in the hall, snickering with him. They'll tease me for the rest of the summer.

When she finished washing her face and hands with the apple-blossom-scented soap that Louise had given her for her birthday, she yanked open the bathroom door and tried to slap her brother, but Dusty escaped and thudded downstairs screaming for Mama, followed by the beastly Ts.

This was Molly's first summer in the community center dance class, and tonight was the first night that lessons and practice would be put aside. This would be a real dance. That meant that the teachers would not choose partners for everyone.

Molly had made the mistake of telling her mother, while they were fixing an early dinner, that she hoped Paul would ask her to dance. Dusty, always eavesdropping, had overheard and was now armed with ammunition that could last him all summer.

"Molly's in love!" he shrieked from the kitchen.

"Hush up or you'll get what's good for you!" Mama cried. "It's too hot for that, Dusty. You and the Ts get out of here."

Molly heard the screen door slam as she crossed the hall into her bedroom, where her pink cotton dress waited for her. Her mother had made it over from an old dress they had found in a trunk in the basement. Molly suspected that it had once belonged to Grandma Donnelly, but she was so grateful to have something new that she pretended it didn't matter.

Through her open window she heard the boys shouting and Mrs. Hawke calling her little boy, Rider. He was only

46

four, too young for Dusty, but he liked watching the older boys. They ignored him elaborately.

Mrs. Hawke and her two children had moved into the Tanakas' house near the end of June, but Mr. Hawke had lived there since the day after Mama finished painting the kitchen. Actually, the Donnellys could have rented the place in any condition because housing was so scarce, but Mama was too proud to do what many people did — turn one set of renters into a dirty house practically on top of the family that was moving out.

It seemed strange to Molly to have anyone but the Tanakas — or Grandma — there. But the Hawkes were nice, and Mr. Hawke worked at the Boeing company, so he rode to work with Dad, Uncle Charlie, and Mr. Barrows.

"Good practice for the time when gas rationing starts," Dad had said gloomily. "We'll end up walking if the war lasts long."

Molly yanked her new dress down over her bony shoulders, watching herself in the mirror. What would Paul think of her?

He'd think that she had grown too much and was now a full inch taller than he, that's what. He'd never ask her to dance.

She was close to tears in anticipation of spending two hours on a hard wooden bench against the wall of the community center gym.

"Are you ready?" Mama asked as she opened Molly's door.

"I guess," Molly said. "Look at me. I'm taller than Paul. I'm taller than anybody in the entire world."

"Well, you're not taller than Louise's brother Bobby," Mama said. "Maybe he'll dance with you."

"No, he won't," Molly said. "He's starting high school and he thinks he's as important as God."

Mama sighed and sat down on the bed. "You exaggerate everything. You're only thirteen. This won't be your last dance."

"First and last," Molly said. "If nobody dances with me tonight, I'll never go again. It's better to have classes, because the teacher makes the boys dance with us."

"Is Louise going?" Mama asked.

"Of course," Molly said.

"Even with her bad leg?"

"She can dance as well as anybody else," Molly said. She lied. Louise had a difficult time, and none of the boys wanted to dance with her. Molly had talked her into taking the class, and she felt obliged to defend her friend. But she knew she wouldn't be alone on that hard bench.

The dance, starting at seven, would end at nine, and so she'd be safe enough walking home in the delicious summer twilight. But Mama had asked Uncle Charlie to pick her up, in spite of her protests — and her unvoiced hope that perhaps Paul Gardner would want to walk her home. Things like that happened in movies. Of course, real life was generally disappointing.

Uncle Charlie and Dad were drinking coffee on the shaded porch when she left.

"I'll see you at nine," Uncle Charlie said.

"Do you have to pick me up?" she asked, keeping an eye on the screen door in case Mama should be listening.

"I'll pick her up," Dad said to his brother, sighing.

"No, I'll do it," Charlie argued. "I want to hear first hand about all the boys who waited in line to dance with Molly."

They talked about Molly as if she were out of earshot! Angry, she stomped down the path.

Mrs. Hawke's daughter, Rachel, leaned against the fence, dreamily watching the street. She gave Molly a wry look as she passed. Molly knew that she'd overheard the conversation on the porch.

"You'll be fine," Rachel said quietly. "Don't worry."

Rachel had just turned seventeen and would be a senior at the high school in the fall. She was taller than Molly and had glossy black hair and beautiful black eyes, and Molly admired her more than she could have said.

"Why don't you come too?" Molly asked suddenly, even though the kids Rachel's age danced at the community center on Saturdays instead of Fridays.

"I don't know how to dance," Rachel said, with astonishing honesty. She didn't seem to be afflicted with vanity.

"You could learn," Molly said. "What will you do when boys ask you to go to the school dances?"

Rachel shook her head and grinned. "I won't be going to dances."

Molly left her there, still watching the street as if she expected to see someone walking toward her. Rachel was mysterious. Molly would have given anything to have been mysterious instead of plain old Molly Donnelly.

The dance was worse than her nightmares. The teacher and the chaperones nagged at the boys to get out on the floor with the girls, but they bunched together in one corner, drinking lemonade and whispering. And snickering. The girls stood stiffly in another corner, pretending they didn't care. Paul didn't show up until twenty minutes before the dance ended, and then he only glanced at Molly and blushed furiously. She felt that he had betrayed her. Or rather, he had betrayed her daydreams, which was even worse. Louise's brother did not show up at all. Daryl Arthur watched through a window, smoking and sneering, but no one wanted him inside.

Louise, watching a stout woman in a flowered dress change records on the record player, said, "I'll never go to another dance as long as I live. I wish I was dead."

Two girls they knew began dancing with each other to a song sung by Frank Sinatra. "We could dance together," Molly said.

"Do you want to?" Louise asked.

"No." Dancing with another girl would only draw attention to her failure, Molly thought.

"I'm going to kill my brother when I get home," Louise whispered. "Mother told him he had to come and dance with me once and then with you."

"I'd just as soon dance with Dusty," Molly said sincerely.

The last record played every Friday was "Good Night, Ladies," and when Molly heard it, finally, she could have shouted with gratitude.

"See you tomorrow morning," Louise said as they walked through the door. "At least we'll have fun at the beach."

Uncle Charlie waited outside with Louise's father. Molly nodded at Charlie and marched toward the car, hoping he wouldn't ask her if she had a good time.

He must have read her mind. "I believe the weather's going to break tomorrow," he said, looking up at the sky. "This has been the hottest July I can ever remember."

She agreed, grateful to discuss weather instead of boys.

But when they reached home, he put out his hand to stop her from leaping out of the car.

"This business of growing up is just about the worst thing that can happen to a person," he said. "It's a big jump to make, getting from childhood to womanhood. Maureen cried herself to sleep for a month after her first dance."

"But Maureen is beautiful," Molly said, not believing him. "I'm not."

"You're more like her than you know," he said.

They sat there in the gathering dark, thinking about Maureen. Her uncle had been told only that the army believed Maureen had been captured by the Japanese in the Philippines. Beyond that, they had heard nothing. He kept in touch with the Polaskis, whose daughter Mary was also presumed to be a prisoner somewhere. All of them hoped for letters that never came.

Finally Molly sighed and opened the car door. "I might as well go in and face them," she said.

"Dusty won't be bothering you," Uncle Charlie said, once more reading her mind. "I had a word with him."

She giggled suddenly, and then turned back to face him, her laughter gone as suddenly as it had come. "Sometimes

I think you're the only friend I've got in this house." she said.

He didn't deny it, the way Mama would have done if she had heard Molly. And he didn't sigh to let her know that she had committed a grave offense by imposing raw emotion on him, the way her father would. He nodded and said, "I remember that feeling, Molly."

"Will it ever get any better?" she asked.

He was silent so long that she was devastated. And then he said, "Living is a lonely journey. Help comes from having landmarks, things to look forward to, traditions. Counting on people — well, that's a risky business. Count on yourself."

She saw her mother push open the screen door and step outside on the lighted porch.

"Let's go in," Charlie said. "Your mama made strawberry shortcake." He lowered his voice and added, "Nobody *needs* to know all the details about tonight, not even me. There's no point in giving people information they can live without."

Mrs. Donnelly asked Molly how she liked the dance, and Molly, mindful of what Uncle Charlie had just told her, smiled and said, "It was fine. I like to dance." And in saying that, she somehow transformed the evening for herself.

She believed she learned a major lesson about life from Uncle Charlie that night. But for the rest of the summer, she avoided the community center on Friday nights.

Louise and Molly started junior high that fall, but it too had changed and was now so crowded that the students attended in shifts. They had English class in one corner of the cafeteria with a group of strangers, the children of war workers who had come to Seattle from all parts of the country. The outsiders made friends among themselves.

One, the thin, dark girl Molly had seen on the beach and mistaken for Emily, lived close to Molly, but they did not walk to school together. There was something so forbidding about Ivy Nickerby's expression that Molly never even said hello to her, and instead walked a careful half a block behind her. As near as Molly could tell, Ivy didn't care.

Paul Gardner was in the second shift, so she seldom saw him. But she wasn't sorry. She couldn't forget he had left her abandoned with her daydreams on that hot July night.

Rationing began. Food, gasoline, heating oil, shoes — all were in short supply.

"Look at these!" Mama said one stormy afternoon as she threw several books of coupons on the kitchen table. She had spent all afternoon standing in line at the post office, waiting to register for the ration books that would allow the family to have its share of the available necessities. "What's your father going to say when he finds out he can only have meat when I've got enough ration points to buy it?"

"Maybe the meat will be better now," Molly said, looking up from her library book. "You've only been able to find hamburger and pork sausage. Now we'll get roast beef like the Barrows family."

"We'll get roast beef only if I do what Dinah Barrows does and pay twice the price to that thief of a butcher," Mama said.

"You wouldn't buy black-market meat, Mama," Molly said, horrified.

"I just might," Mama said. She sat down and propped her elbows wearily on the table. "No, I wouldn't. I don't know how Dinah can do it, what with her brother being in the Marines and shipped out to God knows where. Whenever I think of Maureen . . ."

"We'll hear pretty soon," Molly said, not believing it. Sometimes, in the middle of the night, she woke up in a fright, certain that Maureen had died in the invasion of the Philippines.

"Lord," Mama groaned, "how are we going to heat this great big house all winter if I can only get the amount of oil we used last winter in one month?"

"We'll use the fireplace," Molly said. "Rachel's grandpa brought in a whole truckload of firewood for them. I bet we could get some from him, too."

Mama got to her feet. "That reminds me. I meant to ask Lara Hawke if I could buy eggs from her. She's been getting them from her family's farm. If I crack open one more grocery store egg and find a dead chick in it, I'll give up eating."

While she was at the Hawkes' house, Dad and Uncle Charlie came home. They put their lunch buckets on the counter and poured coffee for themselves from the pot on the back burner of the stove. It wasn't good coffee anymore. Mama used the same grounds over and over. But Dad had stopped complaining after he began adding a generous amount of whiskey to his cup each night.

"Where's Dusty?" Dad asked Molly. "He left his bike in the driveway again."

"I'll put it away," Molly said, closing her book. Doing it herself was easier than arguing with her brother.

"He'll do it," Dad said. He shouted for Dusty, who was upstairs reading comic books with the Ts.

"What's for dinner?" Uncle Charlie asked Molly.

She shrugged. "I don't know. Mama just got home from signing up for our ration books. I don't think she stopped at the store."

"Soup and sandwiches," Uncle Charlie said. "That'll be fine."

Automatically, Molly pulled the bread out of the bread-box. It wasn't sliced — sliced bread was no longer available, although she could not imagine why this was so.

"I think there's some cheese left," she said, sounding every bit as unhelpful as she felt. She hated cooking.

But then, so did Mama.

Mama came back, carrying a bowl full of eggs. "Look what Lara Hawke gave me," she said, all smiles now. "There you are, Joe, Charlie. Look at these wonderful fresh farm eggs. We'll have scrambled eggs for dinner, along with some bacon, if there's any left . . ."

"It's all gone," Molly said.

"What about that sausage?" Mama asked.

"Gone, too. Don't you remember? We had that last night."

Mama blinked and put down the bowl. "How can I cook

when there's nothing left to fix?" she asked of no one in particular.

"Jenny, there are women in Europe who would give their lives for a dozen fresh eggs like you've got there," Dad said. He scowled at her from beneath his eyebrows. That was the most hostility Molly had ever seen him show Mama, but it chilled her.

"Molly and I'll whip us up a feast," Uncle Charlie said. "Eggs, toast, maybe some canned tomatoes."

Dad opened the cupboard door where the whiskey was kept and added more to his cup. Molly turned away and made a great clatter with pans and bowls while Uncle Charlie washed up at the sink. Dad took his whiskey into the living room and turned on the radio. Mama, scowling, went upstairs to their bedroom.

"Don't mind your folks," Uncle Charlie said. "It's the war."

"No, it's not!" Molly said. "It's them."

For Thanksgiving that year, they ate a chicken that Mrs. Hawke gave them. The Donnellys had not been able to find a turkey.

For Christmas dinner, they had meat loaf made of one part hamburger, seven parts oatmeal. Dusty threw a tantrum and refused to touch it. Mr. Donnelly drank himself to sleep after dinner. The house was damp and chilly because they had run out of fuel oil a week earlier and had very little wood left for the fireplace. Mrs. Donnelly, suffering from a cold, went to bed with a hot-water bottle.

Molly and Uncle Charlie sat alone in the living room

with the Christmas tree, a shabby, dry thing that year. But it was decorated with the magical fairy balls and the few remaining strands of tinsel. And the beautiful shell Molly had found on the beach on the day the war started, the shell she was saving for Emily.

"I wonder what Christmas is like in the camp where Emily lives," she said.

"Not as good as ours, I suppose," Uncle Charlie said. "We're lucky people, Molly. We're in our own home, and we don't have to worry about being bombed out of it like the families in England."

But she didn't feel lucky, struggling with stupid little things that became big things because they were so aggravating and persistent.

After Christmas Mama began talking about finding a job at one of the war plants or at a shipyard.

Molly understood that her mother would be happier if she had a job and earned money. She had never been content at home. And anybody would be happier staying away from Dusty. No one could cope with him now. He and the Ts ran with the boys from Tent Town, a collection of tents, trailers, and shacks occupied by war workers who couldn't find housing. The Tent Town children were wild and unsupervised. Molly was frankly afraid of them. But Dusty admired their ways, and he especially admired their freedom.

What would happen to Dusty if Mama went to work? And what would happen to the Donnellys as a family? The results of Mama's intentions were unimaginable to Molly.

"Look at this," Mama cried one evening, waving a sheet of paper in Dad's face. "See what Dusty brought home? Another note from his teacher. He's tardy nearly every day, he sasses her, he throws rocks on the playground. Joe, I don't know what to do with him anymore."

Mr. Donnelly merely reached for the whiskey in the cupboard. It was Uncle Charlie who took Dusty outside and smacked his rear end with the fly swatter, to the astonishment of Molly and her mother. Uncle Charlie didn't believe in spanking children.

But Dusty only minded Uncle Charlie when the man was home. When he was out of sight, Dusty did as he pleased.

Louise's mother had gone to work in November, sewing parachutes in a small factory that had made women's dresses before the war. The Stone family saved the money she earned, hoping to find a used record player for sale somewhere, and a washing machine that was newer than the one they had. Record players and washing machines were not manufactured anymore. Louise's Aunt Shelley had come to live with them and was now in charge of housework and cooking.

"And boy, can she cook," Louise had said once, as she shared her aunt's applesauce cookies with Molly. "She's lots better than my mother."

The Donnellys had no Aunt Shelley to keep house and cook and stand in line endlessly, waiting for meat or coffee or butter or any of the other prizes.

"Maybe we could find a record player somewhere, if I got a job," Mama told Molly one day. "We could have all sorts of things." She was folding the laundry she'd brought up from the basement, and stopped, sighing, to examine a hole in one of Dusty's socks.

"I'll finish putting the laundry away," Molly said, showing how efficient she could be, attempting to head off one of Mama's bad moods.

"I walked up the hill with Rachel today," her mother went on. "She told me that Mrs. Hawke is starting work at the day nursery the church opened. She'll be good at that, but I wouldn't. I want to do something else, something real. I want to work in a factory, and not a parachute factory, either."

"Then I'd have to do everything here," Molly said.

Mrs. Donnelly looked at her appraisingly. "Well, you have to learn sooner or later," she said.

Molly didn't know what her mother was thinking — perhaps she really did believe that Molly could manage alone.

One week later, Mrs. Donnelly began work at a shipyard. On the same afternoon, Molly stood for two hours in line outside the butcher shop, while snow fell several inches deep. When she reached the door at last, the butcher locked it and turned the "Open" sign over to the side that read "Closed."

"You can't do that!" Molly cried, furious and weeping, pounding on the glass with her cold fist.

"He's out of meat now, honey," the woman behind her said. "You'll get used to it."

6

June 1943

There is a line for everything. Two times a week I wait in line at the butcher's. On Saturdays, Mama waits in line to buy cigarettes for Dad and Uncle Charlie. The two of them wait in line for whiskey. Everybody with a car waits in line for gas. Yesterday Louise and I waited in line for two hours to buy pre-war panties with real elastic waists instead of button waists, but the store sold out before we got inside. We'll end up like Mrs. Barrows, when her button came off and she lost her panties at the PTA, or the girl at school who lost hers in front of God and everybody. There is no elastic in anything! I never even thought about elastic before, not in my whole life. Now I pin my panties to my slip, just to be sure. I think I would do almost anything for socks that didn't fall down. I'll bet Emily would laugh if she read this. Maybe I'll show her my journal when she comes back. Darlene gets lots of letters from Frances, her Japanese friend who's in the Idaho camp. Her whole family lives in one room. They don't even have their own bathroom, and they eat with everybody else in a big dining hall. I hope Emily is better off, but I worry that she's not.

By June 1943, the United States had been at war with Japan, Germany, and Italy for a year and a half. Molly had been at war with her brother since February. When they returned from school each day to an empty house, she was expected to take care of him, clean up the kitchen, and shop for food before Mrs. Donnelly got home from the shipyard at five-thirty. At least, this was the routine her mother planned for her. Reality was something else.

Dusty and Molly went to different schools, four blocks apart. Every day she ran from her school to his, to look for him. Nearly every day he either ran off or refused to go home with her, so nearly every day she wasted time hunting him down, pleading with him, and threatening him.

"Why don't you just sock him when you catch him?" Louise asked her one cool June afternoon, after they had been pursuing Dusty for an hour. "Maybe he'd learn something."

"He lied and told Mama that I hit him all the time and she took my allowance away for a month," Molly said. She saw Dusty, ducking around in back of the house where a friend of his lived, and she broke into a run, leaving Louise behind.

She caught him by tricking him, doubling back to reach out and snatch him by the arm when he ran out from behind the woodshed.

He screamed bloody murder, and Molly longed to punch him, but she dared not. She had promised Mama she wouldn't, and her mother knew she wouldn't break a promise.

"Dusty, I've got to go to the store," she said, attempting to make herself heard over his shrieks. "Quit acting like this and come with me. I'll get you some candy, if they've got any."

His friend's mother came out on her porch and called to Molly, her voice sharp with anger. "I wish you'd keep him away from here. He's nothing but trouble."

"Phone my mother tonight and tell her," Molly called back. She meant what she said, but the woman must have thought that Molly was sassing her, because she went back inside and slammed the door hard.

Dusty laughed and twisted free, running off again before Molly could grab him.

Louise, limping worse than ever, caught up with Molly. "Let him go," she said. "I can't do this anymore, honestly. Just tell your mother what a brat he is."

"She knows," Molly said, close to tears. "She says I have to make him mind."

"Why should you be able to when she never could?" Louise asked reasonably.

"I don't know."

"Tell your dad."

Molly turned to stare at Louise. "He won't do anything. He never does. Anyway, he works overtime nearly every night now. Uncle Charlie drives Mr. Hawke and Mr. Barrows home."

"Then how does your dad get home?" Louise asked. She seemed fascinated with Molly's household. Molly gladly would have traded it. The Stones were so organized, so serene, that she was jealous of her friend's life.

"Dad takes the bus," Molly said. She neglected to add that he stopped at the tavern across from the bus stop nearly every night. He and Mama argued about that, but his drinking was only one more problem that never got solved.

Louise and Molly parted company once they came in sight of their school again. Louise lived north of it and Molly lived west. It was too far for Louise to walk her home.

Molly found her house empty, as she knew it would be—Dusty would stay away until Mama came home. Molly gathered the ration books together, along with the grocery money and the list her mother had left, and went out again, heading toward the stores.

Paul Gardner caught up with her a block from the butcher's. "I see you going this way all the time," he said, as he walked his bike beside her.

"I do most of the grocery shopping," she said. She immediately regretted telling him that, for he would guess that her mother was working. Mrs. Gardner, she knew, volunteered her time for several war charities. Her picture had been in the newspapers several times, once showing her in a ball gown. It was not until then that Molly realized the Gardners were rich.

"School's almost out for the summer," Paul said. "Are you and Louise going to the movie with everybody on Class Day?"

Their teachers planned to take the entire eighth grade to a movie on the last day of school. Molly was yearning to go, but her mother, so far, had refused to promise that she'd find somebody else to watch Dusty.

"Louise is going," Molly told Paul, her heart beating in her throat. "I'm not sure yet if I can."

"When will you be sure?" he asked. His clear, light skin was flushed and he looked away from her.

Was he asking her for a Class Day date, she wondered. A date like that would involve riding with him on the bus and sitting next to him in the theater. Several of the girls she knew had already been invited to share in just such an arrangement with some of the more sophisticated boys in eighth grade.

In fact, Daryl Arthur was bragging that he had made Class Day dates with three of the Tent Town girls. This was believable, because the new girls didn't hate him the way that Molly and her friends did.

She decided that she'd better explain her circumstances to Paul, even though she had come to be so ashamed of her brother that she preferred to have people think she was an only child.

"I have to take care of my brother after school," she said, "and unless Mama can find somebody else to do it, I can't go to the movie."

"Can't your neighbors watch him?" Paul asked.

"Mrs. Hawke works at the day nursery," Molly said. "Mrs. Barrows won't watch Dusty. Her own boys are enough work. And we don't know anybody else well enough to ask." The last statement was not strictly true. The other neighbors detested Dusty.

They'd reached the butcher shop. There was no line, which meant that he didn't have anything better than pork sausage or maybe bologna.

Paul got back on his bike. "Well," he said, vague and uneasy, looking anywhere but at her, "I'll see you tomorrow, I guess."

She watched him ride off, knowing that she probably wouldn't see him the next day because he was a second-shift student. What was the use of hoping? She pushed open the door to the butcher shop and joined the women waiting at the refrigerated case. She was right. The only meat available was pork sausage and bologna.

By the time Molly reached her own neighborhood, she was worn out with worry. She hadn't caught a glimpse of Dusty anywhere. She hadn't had time to clean up the kitchen, and Mama was due home in less than an hour. When she saw Rachel walking ahead of her, she called out to the older girl and hurried to catch up. At least Rachel would be company—and she might even offer to carry the sack of vegetables while Molly carried the rest of the food.

Before Molly could ask, Rachel grabbed the sack. "You do all the shopping now?" she asked.

"Most of it," Molly said.

"And you look out for your brother," Rachel added. "Where is he?"

"Home, I hope. He ran off from me again."

Rachel laughed. "He needs a little more of what your uncle Charlie gives him once in a while."

"I know."

Then, without warning, a shower of gravel spattered all over them. Surprised, Molly flinched and dropped her sack.

"Yah, yah!" Dusty screamed from the maple tree that hung over the street. He was halfway up, holding onto a branch. Obviously he'd been waiting for them to pass under it.

Rachel put down the sack she'd been carrying. "That does it," she said. When she stood up, Molly saw that there was blood on her face.

"Now look what you did!" Molly yelled at Dusty.

"I'll handle it," Rachel growled. She hitched up her skirt and climbed the tree so quickly that Molly almost felt sorry for her brother. He was no match for Rachel, who caught the back of his belt and jerked him loose from the branch.

"If you struggle, I'll drop you on purpose," Rachel said, shaking him once as a warning.

Dusty dangled, red-faced, while Rachel worked her way back to the ground. Then, quickly, as soon as she had both feet under her, she knelt, flipped him over her knee, and spanked him.

"That's for hitting me with a rock," she said as she yanked him to his feet. "If you cry, I'll give it to you again because you're a spoiled little snot. And then I'll tell your uncle."

Dusty tore away from her and ran up the hill. But he didn't cry.

Rachel took a handkerchief out of her pocket and dabbed at the cut on her face. "Little monster," she said.

Molly shouted with laughter, but then sobered when she saw Rachel's face. "Does it hurt?" Molly asked.

"I'll live," Rachel said. She examined the blood on the handkerchief and shook her head. "That boy's too much for you. Do you want me to talk to your mother?"

"There isn't anybody else who can watch him," Molly said.

"And summer's coming," Rachel added. "What're you going to do then?"

Molly burst into tears. "I don't know," she said.

Rachel didn't comment on her weeping. Instead, she said, "Somebody's got to give you a hand. I can take care of Dusty this summer. He probably won't like it, but I can manage him. But your mom would have to pay me. I want a summer job to help out with my college expenses."

"You're going to college in the fall?" Molly asked, impressed.

"I want to be a teacher, like my father was," Rachel said.

"But Mr. Hawke works at Boeing," Molly said.

"He's my stepfather," Rachel said. "My dad died when I was a little girl. My name isn't Hawke, it's Chance. I'm Rachel Chance."

"What's Rider's last name, then?" Molly asked.

"He's a Hawke," Rachel said. "He's my half brother, except that I love him like a full brother."

"I wish I could love mine," Molly said.

"Stop blaming yourself," Rachel said. "You didn't make him what he is."

They were passing the Carsons' house, where a new family was moving in. Packing boxes were stacked on the sidewalk and front porch, and a small girl wept bitterly on the bottom step. A frenzied-looking woman counted out money to two elderly men beside the cab of their truck.

"More new people," Molly said. "Mr. Carson was a nice man. It was awful, the way he died when that plane crashed into the packing plant last winter."

"It's always something," Rachel said. "But other people have it worse. People in Europe and England. I guess we ought to be grateful that we've still got houses to live in and our families are together."

"Sure," Molly said. But she thought of Maureen.

And she thought of Emily and her family. Where were they now? Sometimes she did not believe that she would ever see Emily again.

They reached home and found Dusty on the porch with the Barrows twins. Dusty had managed to lose his key again. Molly unlocked the front door, and Dusty ran inside, followed by the Ts.

"I'll come by this evening and talk to your mother," Rachel said. She smiled. "Maybe I can put Dusty to work in my Victory garden."

"You must be joking," Molly said. "Dusty won't even take out the garbage."

"We'll see," Rachel said. She handed Molly the sack she'd been carrying for her. "I can be pretty persuasive."

Rachel's Victory garden was the envy of the neighborhood. The Donnellys owned the vacant lot behind their house, the lot where Uncle Charlie once planned to build a house for Moira and himself and Maureen. But Moira had died, and Uncle Charlie and Maureen moved in with Grandma Donnelly next door. The Donnellys were not handy with gardening, so the vacant lot sat there unused until the Hawkes moved in next door, and Rachel asked if she could use it for a garden, promising to share half of what she raised.

The garden was the source of wonderful surprises, and the Donnellys weren't sorry they had turned the lot over to the tall, strong girl next door.

Molly, who sometimes helped Rachel pull weeds, could not imagine Dusty helping with anything. But she thought the idea was funny enough to share with Uncle Charlie that night, out of the hearing of the rest of the family, of course.

That evening after dinner, Rachel presented herself at the back door and spoke earnestly with Mrs. Donnelly for a good fifteen minutes. Molly, wild with curiosity, spent the time in the living room with Uncle Charlie and Dusty, listening to the radio. When she heard the kitchen door close at last, she waited impatiently for her mother to come and tell everybody the news.

If there was any news. Molly agonized as the minutes ticked by. She would not have put it past her mother to have turned down Rachel's offer.

But at long last, her mother came into the living room, wiping her hands on a towel.

"I wish Joe were home to hear this," she said, "but I guess I'll have to tell him later. I've decided to hire Rachel from next door to watch Dusty this summer—"

"No, no, no!" Dusty shouted. "I hate that girl! I'll run away if she comes here."

"Sit down and shut up, Dusty," Uncle Charlie said. "Now, Jenny, go on with what you were saying."

Dusty, red-faced, sat down, but he glared at Molly as if the scolding had been her fault. She looked away from him, careful not to grin.

"Rachel's older than Molly," Mrs. Donnelly said. "She can keep better track of the boy, and she does need the money. She's starting college in the fall. Isn't that something? Imagine, a little farm girl like her . . ."

"She's not little!" Dusty yelled. "She's bigger than you are. She's big and mean, and I really hate her, Mom. If she takes care of me, she has to take care of Molly, too."

"Molly doesn't need taking care of," Mrs. Donnelly said. "She's fourteen. When you're fourteen, you won't need a baby-sitter—"

"I don't want a baby-sitter!" Dusty screamed.

"I meant housekeeper," Mrs. Donnelly said quickly. "Rachel will be a sort of housekeeper for all of us."

"But what's Molly going to do?" Dusty demanded.

"She'll be helping with the shopping and the housework and everything that Rachel doesn't do," Mrs. Donnelly said.

Dusty sank back in his chair, satisfied. Molly was certain that he was as happy as she was unhappy to hear about all the chores assigned to her.

Summer. She remembered when it had been different. When everything had been different. They'd had a normal life, with Mama home during the day, and Dad coming home on time in the evening, and any kind of food they wanted, and gas to put in the car so that they could go on Sunday drives and picnics. And no scary newsreels in the theaters. And no blue stars hanging in people's windows, signifying that somebody in the family was in the military. And no gold stars, meaning that somebody had been killed. And no long list of dead soldiers and sailors in the paper every single night.

When Emily and her family had lived next door, and "Jap" was a bad word.

When her father came home, it was with bad news. He had been transferred to the night shift, and so he would be sleeping during the day.

"I'll expect you to make an effort to keep Dusty occupied," he told Molly.

"I've hired Rachel to take care of Dusty," Mrs. Donnelly said. She explained the arrangements.

Mr. Donnelly shook his head. "I'll need some quiet around here," he said. "Can't the kids go somewhere else?"

"You mean stay next door at the Hawkes'?" Molly's mother asked.

"You know Dusty won't stay quiet for five minutes at a

71

time," Mr. Donnelly said wearily. He shuffled off to the kitchen, to eat the food kept warm for him in the oven.

"The night shift will mean more money," Uncle Charlie told Mrs. Donnelly. "Look at it that way."

"I'm not staying all day long at the Hawkes'!" Dusty announced.

"You'll do as you're told," Uncle Charlie shouted, exasperated now. He glared at Molly's mother. "Am I the only one around here to see what's happening to this boy? He's worse than the Tent Town kids. It's going to take more than me and Rachel to shape him up. You and Joe have to take a firm stand with him. He's ten years old, for God's sake. Ten! That's plenty old enough to do as he's told without all this damned whining and bellyaching. There's a war on, Jenny! This is no time to raise up a spoiled brat!"

"Yes, there's a war, and he's only a baby," Mrs. Donnelly snapped back.

Uncle Charlie got to his feet and headed toward the stairs. Rachel heard his feet thump on each step, all the way to his room on the third floor.

Mrs. Donnelly stared hard at Molly. "Have you been complaining again?"

"Mama, can't you see what everybody else sees about Dusty?" Molly twisted her fingers together.

"I see that the rest of you are ganging up on him," Mrs. Donnelly said. She left the room, and Molly heard the screen door in the kitchen slam.

Molly climbed the stairs to her room and pushed open the window, then pulled her journal out from under her mattress.

"My family is falling apart," she wrote. "Emily, you were the only one I could ever talk to about things like this. But you've been gone so long that I'm not sure I remember what you look like. And I'm afraid you've forgotten me."

Then she bent her head and wept.

7

June 1943

I can go to the Class Day movie! I'll wear the new
dress Mama found for me at the Bon last Saturday,
Mama's white high-heeled shoes, and an old pair of
silk stockings we found in the trunk Maureen left
behind when she went to the Philippines. I don't
think she would mind, and I'll tell her I borrowed
them as soon as she gets home.

Emily, I wish you were going with us.

Graduating from eighth grade was an important occasion,
but for patriotic reasons Molly's school decided against having a formal graduation ceremony at night and wasting
electricity. Instead, a morning assembly was planned. Parents were invited, of course, but not many of the students
Molly knew had parents who were free to come. Nearly
everyone was working now, and no one got a day off for
anything but the most serious reasons—a son or brother
dying in the war, for instance.

"Who cares if our folks can't come?" Louise asked, minutes before the ceremony was to begin. She and Molly were combing their hair in the girls' lavatory, taking turns at the mirror with the other girls and worrying about how they looked. "My father hates coming to school for any reason—he says it reminds him of how much he hated it when he was young—and Mom said that high school graduation ceremonies are the important ones."

"But still," Molly said, "I wish my family could have come."

"You could always call the grade school and see if they'll let Dusty run over," Louise said. She elbowed Molly, laughing. "Wouldn't that be fun?"

"I'd rather fall down stairs," Molly said. "But thanks to Rachel, at least I can go to the movie this afternoon. Listen, does my lipstick look all right? I wish I'd bought the darker color. This hardly shows."

Lipstick was allowed on Class Day, and all the girls were wearing it. Some of the Tent Town girls were wearing even more makeup: mascara, eyebrow pencil, and color on their cheeks. This had been absolutely forbidden, and both Molly and Louise were waiting, with considerable pleasure, for the Tent Town girls to be caught.

"You know why I can't stand those Tent Town girls?" Louise had once asked Molly. "I'm afraid that my mom is right—they won't be going home after the war."

Their dislike of the outsiders was returned enthusiastically. And it especially galled Molly to see how much attention Paul Gardner got from the brazen girls from other parts of the country, girls with strange accents and clothes that were too grown-up for eighth-graders in Seattle.

Emily, who had also been born somewhere other than Seattle, had not been a bold, flamboyant girl with a loud voice and bad manners. What would she think of these unpleasant strangers? Was she, also, trying to deal with the unfamiliar ways of people she did not like very much? Molly resolved to write the question in her journal so that she would remember to ask Emily when she returned to Seattle.

Molly and Louise pushed their way through the crowd in the lavatory, walking awkwardly on their high heels, watching their feet self-consciously.

"I wish Mama had bigger feet," Molly said. "These shoes are so small that I think my toes must be folded in half by now. But we didn't have a shoe coupon left, thanks to my brother. He actually lost his new shoes! At least, that's what he says. I think he threw them away somewhere, because I know that he hated them. He wanted brown and all the store had was black."

"You can take your mother's shoes off in the movie," Louise said. "Unless Paul sits next to you."

"He won't," Molly said, miserable now that Louise had reminded her that Paul had never asked to pay her bus fare or buy her movie ticket, and so she did not have a Class Day date.

"Paul will sit with a bunch of other boys, and they'll yell and clap at all the wrong times," she added.

She would be embarrassed by his behavior if he did

those things, and she would end up wondering why she liked him—and those feelings of distaste were worse than the disappointment she felt because he wasn't her Class Day date. She had written several essays in her journal about these strange, conflicting emotions, but she could not even begin to understand them.

The girls idled in the hall; it was too early to go to class, too late to invent a reason to return to the locker they shared.

"I'm not sure I want to leave this school and go to high school," Louise said suddenly.

"Neither do I," Molly said. "The high school is too big. It's full of strangers." She plucked at the front of her dress, not certain now if she liked its small rose-colored print.

Clothes were hard to find, especially for people who wore common sizes. Molly and her mother had rushed through nearly every department store in downtown Seattle, looking for something that was suitable for Class Day and would fit Molly. This was the only dress they could agree upon. They had argued bitterly in Fredericks about a somber gray dress with white cuffs that Molly had thought looked like a uniform. Remembering the argument angered Molly all over again. Her mother did not have time for her anymore. Not that she'd ever been like Louise's mother, who doted on everything Louise did or said.

Paul passed and smiled briefly at them, but Molly could not tell if he had directed his smile at her or at Louise.

"He'll sit with you," Louise predicted.

"No, he won't," Molly said, crossing her fingers behind her back and hoping she was wrong. "He won't."

But he did. Molly and Louise had found seats in the theater near the center, and Molly had forgotten about Paul, momentarily at least. She and Louise sat down and turned to talk to the girls behind them when Molly was aware that someone had slipped into the seat beside her. She turned to look, and it seemed to her that her heart stopped.

"Hi," Paul said, and he cleared his throat. Another boy was with him, sitting on his other side. Tall, gentle Henry Green.

"Hi Paul, hi Henry," Molly said. She was afraid that they had heard her gasping. It was difficult to breathe in such a crowded place. The whole eighth grade was there, making more racket than the monkeys at the zoo. And she was terrified, now that her big moment had come.

Louise nudged her and covered her smile with one hand. The girls behind them fell silent out of respect for the situation.

The curtain rose and the movie began, starring Louise's favorite actor, Dennis Morgan. The audience cheered, and Molly sank back in her seat.

It was impossible to concentrate on the musical. While she appreciated the songs, she was so aware of Paul's presence that the plot escaped her. He leaned on the armrest between their seats, never looking away from the screen. He smelled so good, like freshly washed cotton and soap.

And then, near the end of the movie, he put his arm around her.

She heard the girls behind her suck in their breath. Louise turned to look at them. One of them must have pointed at Molly, because Molly realized that Louise was studying her. Carefully, gently, Louise nudged her foot while she watched the screen.

Molly had no idea what to do. Should she lean slightly toward Paul, to make it easier for him to keep his arm around her? Or should she continue sitting straight upright? Should she look at him? Smile? Or was it proper to frown a little, indicating that she was a very nice girl and his gesture was not completely welcome? But what if he took his arm away then?

And never did it again? Never, in all this world?

She caught herself wringing her hands, which were now damp with perspiration. On the screen, the desert sheik kissed the red-haired heroine, and Paul squeezed her shoulder a little, almost imperceptibly.

Panicked now, Molly leaned forward and made a great fuss over straightening her dress over her knees.

When she leaned back again, Paul's arm was gone. Molly could have wept with disappointment.

When the movie was over, Paul and Henry walked up the aisle behind Molly and Louise. It was impossible to talk in the lobby, which was jammed with people. Outside, Molly stood awkwardly, waiting for Paul to catch up to her. When he did, all he said was, "I'll see you—in high school, I guess."

And then he and blushing Henry disappeared into the crowd.

Molly looked away and yanked Louise by the hand. "Let's go home."

"Wasn't the movie wonderful?" Louise asked. "Isn't Dennis Morgan good-looking? Don't you like his voice? Doesn't he make a good sheik?"

"What?" Molly turned her head to stare at her friend. "Oh, yes."

"What's wrong? Are you sad because Paul didn't offer to go home on the bus with us?"

"That would be dumb," Molly said. "Why would he do something like that?"

"Because he's crazy about you," Louise said. "I don't know why he didn't come along with us. Henry could have come, too."

"Then they'd have to take the bus back to town and transfer to their own buses," Molly explained. "You know that. They live a long way from us."

"A mile or so," Louise said, scoffing. "They could have walked home."

Molly turned on her. "Are you rubbing it in?"

"No!" Louise exclaimed. "I didn't mean it like that. But he ought to have gone home on the bus with you. I guess he didn't because he knew I'd be there. I'm sorry, Molly. I spoiled everything for you."

"No, you didn't," Molly said. But privately, she pretended to herself that Louise was the reason Paul had not gone home with her on her bus.

Of course, it was just as well. What would he have found at her house? Her father was sleeping and would have been furious if she had asked Paul to come inside with her. The house was hot and untidy. And Dusty would have noticed when she came home and charged over from the Hawkes' and acted like a brat.

"After we get off the bus," Molly said, "let's stop at the drugstore and have chocolate-flavored Cokes. My treat."

"No, my treat," Louise said. "I got an advance on my allowance, so we can have doubles."

Molly pushed Paul out of her mind when they boarded the bus. They took seats in the back, and once they were seated, Molly saw Ivy Nickerby sitting across the aisle. The tall, slender girl had been at the theater, too, with no special friend. Ivy didn't seem to have any friends. She was as solitary as she had been when she first moved to Seattle.

Molly and Louise said hello to her, but Ivy only nodded in return. Louise looked at Molly and rolled her eyes.

They would all get off at the same stop. A new problem presented itself. Should they invite Ivy to the drugstore with them? There was no way Molly could tactfully whisper the question to Louise now.

When they got off the bus at their stop, the problem did not go away, for Ivy turned in the direction of the drugstore too. And she went in the door ahead of them.

Molly looked to Louise for guidance. Louise shrugged.

Ivy sat at one of the small metal tables near the soda fountain and put her purse on the floor, then sat back and pushed her dark hair away from her face.

To ignore her was more than Molly and Louise could

manage. Molly did not particularly want to make friends with Ivy because there was something about her, a sense of barely concealed misery, that served as a barrier.

"What . . ." Molly whispered.

"Should we?" Louise whispered.

Molly shrugged and walked to the table. "Can we sit with you?" she asked. "Would you like company?"

"I don't care if I have it or not," Ivy said. She didn't smile, but she did lift her delicately arched eyebrows.

Molly realized, with surprise, that Ivy was beautiful.

Louise pulled out a chair first and plopped awkwardly into it. "Do you come in here often?" she asked Ivy.

"After school, sometimes," Ivy said.

Molly sat down and pulled the soda fountain menu out of its metal rack. She knew it by memory, but she needed something to do. "What are you going to have, Louise?" she asked.

"I thought we decided on chocolate Cokes," Louise said, sounding surprised.

Molly's face burned. "I forgot." She put the menu back.

Old Mr. Pearson, who owned the drugstore and had to wait on customers because he could no longer find anybody else to do it, limped over and took their orders, then waited while Ivy studied the menu.

"I'll have a strawberry sundae," Ivy said finally. She did not look up at either Mr. Pearson or the girls sitting with her.

After the old man left, Louise said, "How did you like the movie, Ivy?"

For the first time they saw her smile. "It was wonderful," she said. "I love musicals. I try to see every one that comes to town at least twice."

Molly and Louise exchanged an amazed look. The transformation in Ivy was remarkable, as if a light had gone on behind her eyes.

"Next year, in high school, you should sign up for the choir," Louise said. "Molly and I want to do that."

"I plan on it," Ivy said. "I can hardly wait."

"You like to sing?" Molly asked.

Their orders came and they waited until Mr. Pearson limped away before they continued. "I like everything about music," Ivy told them.

"Molly used to take piano lessons, before the war," Louise said. "She's got a grand piano in her music room."

Ivy looked up briefly, then back at her ice cream. "I still take piano lessons."

"Where?" Molly asked. "My teacher was drafted and my mother couldn't find another for me."

"Mine teaches at the music school during the day," Ivy said. "But at night she takes pupils in her home."

Molly blinked. When her mother had suggested calling the school to find a teacher for Molly, Molly had discouraged her. She was certain that she was not good enough to have a teacher from such an exotic place. And she had heard that people had to audition. Ivy must be a wonderful musician.

"I'll bet you're really good," she said, working hard to keep the envy out of her voice.

Ivy shrugged. "I only take piano lessons so that I ca[n] accompany myself when I sing."

Molly sipped her Coke. Ivy was impressive. Who woul[d] have thought that such a quiet, strange girl had all thi[s] talent?

"Is your dad a musician? Or your mother?" Louis[e] asked.

"My dad works at the shipyard," Ivy said. She hesitate[d] a moment and looked down at her ice cream, now melting "My mother is a singer," she said finally.

"Really?" Louise squealed. "Who is she? Have we hear[d] of her? Does she sing with a band?"

Ivy stirred the melted ice cream in her bowl. "She doesn'[t] sing anymore."

"But why not?" Louise demanded.

Molly sensed something wrong, and she nudge[d] Louise's ankle.

"My mother . . ." Ivy began. She shook her head an[d] looked out the drugstore window. "My mother is i[n] Holland."

"What's she doing there?" Louise exclaimed. "The Ger[-] mans are in Holland!"

Ivy's hand stirred the melted ice cream, but she sti[ll] looked out the window. "She went there before the war, t[o] get her grandmother and bring her here to live with u[s]. She wasn't doing very well alone. But the war started, an[d] they couldn't leave."

"You mean they're trapped there?" Molly asked. He[r] mouth was dry. She was horrified.

Ivy's spoon clinked in the glass bowl. Around and around it went.

"We don't really know if they are still in Holland," she said quietly. "They might be somewhere else now."

"But where else would they be?" Louise asked. "You mean they're trying to come here? How could they do that? Nobody except soldiers and sailors can travel across the ocean now."

This was a terrible conversation. Molly kicked Louise, hard, and Louise sat back, startled, gawking at her.

"My great-grandmother is a Jew," Ivy said. "They're probably in a relocation camp." She watched the street outside the window. Her hand slowed and she put aside her spoon.

"You mean like the Japanese here?" Louise asked, glaring at Molly. She had moved her feet out of Molly's reach.

Ivy looked at Louise soberly. "Something like that," she said.

"We have a friend—Emily Tanaka—who went to a camp here, but she'll be back when the war is over," Molly blurted. "Everything will be fine then."

"Yes," Ivy said. "When the war is over."

Molly was saturated with misery. What was wrong with Louise that she would keep on and on about something? Didn't she realize that the camps in Europe could not be like the camps here? The Nazis didn't care what happened to anybody.

She dragged the conversation back to music with difficulty, for she could tell that Louise wanted to ask more questions. Shortly afterward, Ivy said goodbye to them and left. She didn't say anything about seeing them again.

"Louise, how could you have done that?" Molly whispered savagely.

"What are you talking about?" Louise cried. "Why did you kick me? And on my bad leg, too."

"Can't you imagine what happens to people who are put in the Nazi camps?"

The color drained out of Louise's face. "You mean she thinks her mother and the old lady are dead, don't you?"

"Maybe." Molly pushed her unfinished Coke away from her. "Maybe. I hate this war."

That night, late, she and Uncle Charlie sat on the back porch.

"Nice big moon tonight," Uncle Charlie said.

"Yes."

"Did you have a good time at the movies?" he asked. "I know that you said you did at the dinner table, but now I want to know the whole story. Did you, honestly?"

Molly remembered Paul's arm around her and she blushed in the dark. "It was fine. I'd like to see the movie again."

"What did you and Louise do afterward? Go out for sodas with your boyfriends?"

Molly laughed. "You know we don't have boyfriends."

"What?" Uncle Charlie exclaimed. "I've been saving my money to get you a nice engagement present the minute you finish high school, when you and what's-his-name set the date."

Molly rested her head on her knees. "Uncle Charlie, what happens to Jews in places like Holland?"

Silence. She raised her head and saw her uncle looking across the back yard, toward the place where the willow tree drooped silvered leaves over the goldfish pond.

"Uncle Charlie?"

"I expect that they have a hard time," he said. "Hitler doesn't like Jews. He made that clear years ago. I don't know why nobody listened to him until it was too late."

"Lots of people here don't like Japanese," Molly said. "People like Mrs. Barrows. She was glad when the Tanakas were put in a camp. I suppose it was the same thing in Holland, don't you think?"

"It's not a nice world," Uncle Charlie said, and he cleared his throat. "Say, listen here, girl, I've been meaning to ask you something."

"What's that?"

"Well, it's not exactly my question, it's Father O'Hara's. He wants to know if you're considering maybe taking the plunge, now that you're old enough to think the matter through."

"You mean become Catholic?" Molly asked. "That's one of the things I intend to decide during vacation."

"I see," Uncle Charlie said. "You have so many important matters on your mind that you have to give them appointments."

Molly laughed and leaned against his shoulder. "Confirmation is over with for this year. Anyway, I'd feel like an idiot going through it with the little kids. That's what I'll be thinking about—if I can get through it when I'm ten feet taller and a million years older than everybody else."

"That's it?" Uncle Charlie asked. "You're worried about being the oldest one?"

"Maybe there's more," Molly said slowly. She leaned back and looked up at the moon floating in the deep sky. "Maybe I feel that the only time I really believe in God is when I'm in church or when I'm saying the rosary. I can't . . . I can't just *believe*."

"'Lord, I believe; help thou mine unbelief.'"

"Do you suppose God will like me even if I can't join a church?" Molly asked. "Because I'm not sure I'll be able to do that."

Uncle Charlie leaned his chin against her hair. "I think that you make Him dance with joy, Molly Donnelly. And I know for a fact that you make Him laugh."

"Has He started answering you at last?" Molly asked, and then, before he could reply, she jumped up and ran inside.

His laughter rang out over the dark neighborhood.

8

August 1943

Mrs. Barrows's brother, Denny, was killed fighting in the Pacific. They have changed the blue star in their window to a gold one. No one has seen Mrs. Barrows since they got the news, and the shades are down all the time. The Ts told Dusty that she stays in bed all day. When Mama visited, Mrs. Barrows wouldn't let her in, and she screamed something about the Tanakas. Mama left a hot casserole with a whole pound of hamburger in it and said that's all she's going to do—she said Mrs. Barrows ought to pull up her socks and get on with things, because we still have to win the war. Uncle Charlie asked Father O'Hara to say a mass for Denny. Denny is the only man I know who has been killed. So far, anyway.

   Louise and I are going to pick string beans for a farmer who can't get help anymore. We'll earn lots of money for school clothes, if we can find any to buy.

The August sun burned white in a colorless sky, and with every step Molly took, white dust rose around her ankles. Her wicker basket was only half filled with string beans. Louise, lagging far behind in the next row, had stopped and was sitting on the ground, mopping her scarlet face.

A narrow dirt road separated two sections of the bean field. On the north side, the farmer's family, including several cousins, picked busily. They made frequent trips back to the shed, and their pay tickets were punched again and again, recording the number of baskets they delivered.

But on the south side, matters were different. That section was dotted with perspiring, struggling pickers who were gleaning, working in the rows that had already been picked by the farmer's family, searching for beans that had been missed. The day was half over, and Molly had turned in only one basket so far. She doubted that she would find enough beans to fill another. Louise had yet to fill even one.

At noon the farmer, his hairy belly bulging between his tattered undershirt and leather belt, hammered a bell with a metal rod. From all directions, dusty pickers walked slowly toward the single water faucet in the field. There was no point in hurrying, for the farmer's family had first turn at the water, and everyone else had to wait. And wait. Molly and Louise had learned this at ten o'clock, during the first water break.

Molly dropped her basket in the row and shuffled to the road. Louise followed, clumsily re-tying her scarf so that it would keep sweat out of her eyes. Another girl, a year or two older than they, trudged toward Molly, herding ahead of her three little sisters. One was openly weeping, scrubbing her fists in her eyes and muddying her face with dust and tears.

"I'm never coming back here," Penny Shellkirk said, her face flushed with anger. "Nobody told us that we'd be gleaning instead of picking fresh rows." She bent and hugged the weeping girl, who clutched at her with dirty fingers.

"We've got hours and hours left to work before the bus takes us back to Seattle," Molly said. "If it weren't so far, I'd leave now."

"The farmer owns that old bus," Penny said bitterly. "It goes when he tells it to, and I bet it won't leave until dark tonight."

"But it's supposed to leave at five!" Molly protested.

Louise staggered up then, and the conversation had to be repeated for her. She burst into tears, and Penny's little sister, astonished, stopped her own crying to stare.

"I can't bear working until nine—or even later," Louise cried. "This is double daylight saving time, Molly. We could be here forever. I'll never get my basket full, and I haven't earned enough money to pay for lunch."

"Didn't you bring your own lunches?" Penny asked. "You wouldn't buy lunch from the farmer!"

"The ad in the paper said he'd give us lunch for a small charge," Molly said.

"Small charge!" Penny hooted. "It'll cost you a whole dollar, that's what. And all you'll get is two slices of bread and a wormy carrot."

"I'm so hungry I'd eat anything, but I've only earned thirty cents," Molly said. "Louise hasn't earned anything yet."

"Haven't you ever picked before?" Penny asked.

Molly and Louise shook their heads.

"This is my third time," Penny said. "The first time, I fell for that stuff about getting lunch for a small charge. Now we bring our own. But we've never gleaned before. I'd heard about it, but I didn't believe it. Now I wish I had. My sisters don't earn much, but they can't earn anything gleaning. It's not fair."

"That's the truth," a stout woman said. Her name was Ellen, and she waited with them, mopping her face with a dirty handkerchief. "I asked before I got on the bus if this was picking or gleaning, and the driver told me that it would be picking. Isn't that right, Sophy?"

Another woman joined them. Horrified, Molly saw that her nose was bleeding.

"I can't take this heat," Sophy said. "I just can't take it. I'll have to leave."

"How will you get back to town?" Molly asked, determined that she and Louise would go with her. Enough was enough.

"Hitchhiking is the only way," Sophy said, blotting her nose with a bloodstained handkerchief. "It's not bad. There are always trucks heading toward town. If we're lucky, we can catch a feed truck going back empty. There'll be room for all of us."

"Are we going home?" the weeping child asked Penny. "Please, Penny, are we going home?"

"You bet," Penny said, sounding suddenly furious. "But not before I tell that fat farmer a thing or two."

"Don't waste your breath, honey," Ellen called after her. "He can load up another busload of patriotic suckers tomorrow."

Molly watched while Penny stormed toward the farmer, saw her angry gestures, saw the farmer laugh.

"Wait a minute, Louise," she said. "I'll ask for my money before we leave. He owes me thirty cents, and I want it."

But getting it was not so simple. The farmer's wife explained that no one got paid until the end of the day, when the "pay wagon" drove out from the house.

"You don't think I'd carry money out here on the field with all of you hanging around, do you?" she said. Her eyes glinted with malice. "I don't even know who you are. You could have come here straight out of reform school. Or you could be one of those girls who pick up sailors on Skid Road."

Sickened, Molly turned away. She pulled her cardboard ticket out of her pocket and threw it on the ground.

"Didn't you get your money?" Louise asked when Molly was close enough to hear her.

Molly shook her head. "Come on, let's go. We'll start toward the highway now, and the others can catch up with us. I can't stand being here one second longer."

It was too hot to talk. The girls struggled down the rough dirt road to the line of dusty poplars that marked the edge of the highway. Once Molly looked back and saw Penny and her sisters far behind, walking with Sophy and Ellen.

"There ought to be somebody we can complain to about this," Molly said disgustedly.

"Everybody will only tell you there's a war on," Louise said. "My dad said that some farmers try to do their best, but others get rich by cheating the people they hire and then selling their crops on the black market."

Molly wiped sweat out of her eyes. "I'm so thirsty I could die," she said.

Louise stopped and picked up two pebbles. "Here," she said, handing one to Molly. "Put this in your mouth and push it around with your tongue. You'll make spit that way."

Molly shouted with laughter, but she put the pebble in her mouth. Louise was right.

"Where did you learn that?" she asked, the pebble clicking against her teeth.

"I read it in a book," Louise said. "If we don't get a ride back to town, and it looks like we'll starve to death, I know how to snare a rabbit with a string. I learned that in a book, too."

"That's horrible!" Molly cried. Suddenly both girls were laughing so hard that they spit out their pebbles to keep from choking on them.

"I'll remember this day as long as I live," Louise said, panting.

"I'm afraid that I will too," Molly said, and the girls laughed again, staggering against each other.

The others caught up with them, and reluctantly, one by one, they joined in the laughter. Molly looked back and saw the farmer and his family staring after them.

"Wave goodbye," Molly said. "Quick, while they're still watching."

All but Sophy waved. Sophy made a gesture that Molly had only seen made by Tent Town boys and Daryl Arthur.

The laughter began again, and the small band of exhausted, dusty pickers was helpless to control it. A truck stopped almost immediately, and a white-haired old man stuck his head out the open window.

"I hope you folks want a ride, because I need to hear a joke right about now," he said. "I just blew out a tire and put on my spare, and I won't be getting another until the war's over. Make me laugh at that if you can."

But he was already laughing. He got out of the truck cab, helped everyone into the back, and then started toward Seattle.

"Oh, my God," Ellen exclaimed, sagging against Sophy. "If I can live through this, I can live through anything. Tomorrow we'll try to find a tomato farmer, if you're up to it, Sophy."

"I'd rather die," Sophy said, and this set off the laughter again.

Molly and Louise gave up the idea of helping the war effort by picking crops. Collecting newspapers and tin cans with Dusty and the Ts was easier.

Rachel was responsible for Dusty and the Ts working hard collecting scrap metal, paper, rubber, and fat. She gave them a choice. They could either work in her Victory garden or join the community center's scrap drive, where they would be out from under her merciless supervision for a few hours each day and under the more benevolent eyes of three elderly women.

Rachel told this to the Donnellys, out of Dusty's hearing, and added, "They get points for the stuff they collect, so that's why they work so hard. At the end of summer, the kid with the most points gets a war bond and his picture in the paper with the mayor."

"Sounds good to me," Molly said.

"You're too old to win the prize," Rachel said. "But they'd appreciate your help, all the same."

So Louise and Molly finished the summer by scraping small cans of pork fat into large tins and loading the nasty mess into the back of a truck that carried everything away from the community center once a week.

"I've changed my mind about wishing summer could last forever," Louise said one day.

"Me too," Molly said. She wiped her hands on a greasy towel and wrinkled her nose. "Anything is better than this."

"I'll never eat pork again," Louise said.

"Or string beans," Molly added.

"Have a pebble," Louise said, and both girls laughed.

What would Emily think of this? Molly wondered. She had such a good sense of humor. Would she have laughed with us in the bean field? And here?

I'll remember to tell her, Molly thought. I'll write it all down in my journal.

Something strange was going on with Uncle Charlie. He had gone out five Saturday evenings in a row, instead of walking to the movies with the rest of the family. Molly had asked him outright what he was doing, but never got an acceptable answer.

"I've taken up folk dancing at the community center," he said one evening, when they were sitting on the porch again, enjoying the hint of autumn in the clear air.

"You hate dancing," Molly countered.

"I'm dating a beautiful widow named Vanessa Consuela Billingsbarrow," Charlie said.

"There is nobody in the entire world named Vanessa Consuela Billingsbarrow," Molly said. "But I wish you would meet a nice widow, somebody you could take along with us on Saturdays when we go to the movies."

"Listen, young lady, if I knew a nice widow, I wouldn't take her along with you people to the neighborhood movies. No, sir, I'd take her downtown to the Fifth Avenue, or maybe the Rivoli . . ."

"The Rivoli is a burlesque theater, Charlie," Molly said. "You wouldn't take a nice widow there."

"Maybe I don't want a nice widow," Charlie said. "Maybe I want a naughty widow, one who wears a red dress with those sparkling things on it."

Molly laughed and nudged him. "I bet that's it. I'll tell Mama."

Charlie threw his arm around her shoulders. "Don't you dare! Jenny will have the hide off me. She's saving me for Mrs. Barrows, as soon as Mr. Barrows throws himself off a bridge to get away from her."

"Things were better around here when Mrs. Barrows

was still feeling so bad about Denny," Molly said, sober now.

"She's a witch and a half, that one," her uncle said.

It wasn't until later, when Molly was writing in her journal, that she realized that Uncle Charlie had once more successfully evaded answering her question about his Saturday nights.

On the first Saturday in September, Father O'Hara came to the house with Mr. and Mrs. Polaski.

Molly heard the doorbell from the kitchen, where she was carefully pressing the new skirt she planned to wear on the opening day of high school.

"Get the door, Molly," her mother said as she wiped up spilled juice from the counter, where two dozen jars of peaches sat cooling. Uncle Charlie and Dad were busy in the basement, cleaning out the furnace ducts for winter. Dusty had left after lunch for the Ts' house.

Molly was astonished to see the visitors, who never came without phoning first.

"Is Charlie here?" Father O'Hara asked.

Molly saw Mrs. Polaski's swollen eyelids and Mr. Polaski's trembling hands. "What's wrong?" she asked quickly.

"We need to see Charlie," Father O'Hara said. His eyes suddenly flooded with tears.

Molly screamed for Charlie, and everyone came running.

They stood together in the living room, staring into each other's faces.

"Why are you here?" Mrs. Donnelly asked.

"We need to speak to Charlie alone," Father O'Hara said.

"This is my family," Charlie said. "What the hell's going on, Pete? You're scaring us."

Father O'Hara looked at Mrs. Polaski, who sobbed suddenly. The priest touched her hand and she bit her lip.

"We've had a letter from Mary," she said.

"A letter!" Charlie shouted. "You've had a letter from Mary? Is she all right? Where is she?"

"We don't know where she is," Mr. Polaski said. "The letter doesn't say much." He cleared his throat.

Mrs. Polaski took a dirty piece of paper from her purse and unfolded it carefully. She looked at Father O'Hara for guidance, and he nodded.

"I'll read it to you, Charlie," she said. "That would be easiest. There's no date on it, or if there was, it was torn off. It says, 'Dear Mom and Dad, I'm in a camp and feeling fine. Hope you do, too. Had a party for my twenty-seventh birthday. Judy, Bonita, and Carrie send their love. Maureen is with Moira.' And it's signed, 'Your loving daughter, Mary.'"

The room was so silent Molly could hear the dining room clock tick.

"Judy, Bonita, and Carrie, they were the nurses at the hospital with Mary and Maureen," Charlie said slowly. "Maureen wrote to me about them."

Mrs. Donnelly sobbed, a strangled, harsh sound. Molly's father gripped her arm.

"There wasn't a nurse named Moira there," Charlie said. "I'd have remembered, because that was Maureen's mother's name."

"We can't be sure about anything, Charlie," Father O'Hara said. "Someone named Moira could have transferred there before the war broke out. You'll have to wait for the army . . ."

"How did you get this letter?" Uncle Charlie asked quietly.

"It came in the mail, just like a regular letter," Mr. Polaski said. "Show him the envelope, honey."

Mrs. Polaski took an envelope from her purse, dirty, stained, folded over several times, bearing an American stamp.

"How can this be?" Uncle Charlie asked. "It looks like it's been all over the world. But it's got an American stamp."

"Sometimes guards are bribed and letters are smuggled out," Father O'Hara said. "No one wants to investigate, because then the underground post office might be cut off. You're right—this letter probably has been all over the world before it reached the United States and someone finally trusted it to a regular post office."

"Mary mentions her birthday," Charlie said. "When would that have been?"

"October 17," Mrs. Polaski said. Tears gushed down her face now. She made no effort to stop them.

"This is September," Charlie said. "That's eleven months back. All this time my girl was dead and I didn't know it. I was always sure I'd feel it in my bones if she died."

"This letter doesn't prove she's dead," Mama said. "Why didn't Mary come straight out and say it if it was true? Why would she write that Maureen was with Moira?"

"If the letter had fallen into the wrong hands, she could have been punished for making the camp sound bad or dangerous," Father O'Hara said.

"If the Japanese want the camp to sound like a vacation, why don't they let the prisoners send letters directly to us?" Mama cried. "Not even the Red Cross can get word out from most of them. Who are they trying to fool?"

Father O'Hara patted Mrs. Donnelly's shoulder. "It's their way. It puts more pressure on people."

"It's barbaric!" Mama shouted. "We can't believe this letter! We can't give up!"

Uncle Charlie put his arms around her and said, "Mary may have risked her life to send us this word. We'll believe it."

Then he turned away and walked out of the room. They listened to his feet climb the stairs to the third floor.

"Thank you for coming," Mrs. Donnelly told the Polaskis. "Thank you, too, Father. It was good of you to bring the news. We're so glad that Mary and the other girls are—"

"Oh, God, I would rather have died than tell you this," Mrs. Polaski cried. "It was the men that made me do it."

"We had to know," Mrs. Donnelly said. "Charlie had to know. It wouldn't have been fair to let him go on believing that she'd be coming home some day."

The Polaskis left, and Father O'Hara stood uncomfortably blinking, adjusting his glasses, sighing.

Finally, to break the misery, Molly said, "Charlie and I'll be seeing you tomorrow morning, just like always, Father O'Hara."

The priest nodded. "If there's anything I can do, you'll call, won't you?"

"We will," Mr. Donnelly said.

The priest left, and Molly turned to her parents. "Did you honestly think Maureen was coming home?"

They looked at each other and then at their daughter.

"We tried to believe it," her mother said. "Because Charlie did."

"Where is God supposed to be when things like this happen?" Molly asked, her voice harsh. "Charlie believes in God, you know. He really does. He's not like me. So where is God now?"

"Charlie would tell you that He's the same place He was when His own child died," Molly's father said.

Molly turned away from him and shook her head. "Words," she said. "Just words. If there is a God, He doesn't care."

"But you go to church anyway," her mother said.

Molly looked back at her. "I'm like the two of you," she said. "I try to believe because Charlie *does* believe."

She struggled to find the words she needed to say. "Charlie is like the little wheels and things in a clock," she said. "He's what makes this family keep the right time. He loves all of us and we love him. The rest of us, we all come and go by ourselves, as if we aren't even related anymore. Charlie is what makes us work. Without him, we wouldn't be much more than strangers, like the people I met in the bean field."

"What a horrible thing to say!" Molly's mother cried. "How dare you! I ought to slap your sassy face for that."

But she didn't. Molly would have been relieved if her mother had struck her, if something—anything!—happened to cause a pain sharp enough to take her mind off Maureen.

But there was no relief from it, no distraction. Late that evening, Molly took out her journal and wrote, "I try not to think about Maureen, but I do. It's like having a bruise on my soul. I would give anything to be a little girl again."

Charlie did not go out that night. Molly heard him walking upstairs, from one end of his long room to the other, over and over. The light from his window fell on the tall birch tree until morning.

9

January 1944

A year ago this month Seattle had the worst snow-
storm anybody could remember. This year the
daffodil bulbs are already sprouting. It was so nice
yesterday that Louise and I walked to the beach, but
afterward we were sorry we did. We saw another
hospital ship coming in.

Uncle Charlie goes to the military hospital two
nights a week, and he says it's so crowded now that
there are beds in the hall. At school, there's a list of
dead graduates hanging in the main hall. Every
month it gets longer. Our algebra teacher's son was
killed and his name is there. Sometimes we see the
teacher looking up at the name. His son died on his
nineteenth birthday.

My cousin Frank is nineteen now and stationed in
England. Once he sent me a V-mail letter, but nearly
everything he wrote was blacked out by the censor.
Poor Frank—he always did talk a lot.

Molly and Louise settled themselves down in the last row of the soprano section in choir. Directly behind them, separated by an aisle, Paul Gardner and Henry Green sat in the first row of the tenor section. All of this came about at the request of Mr. Prescott, the music director, but Louise and Molly firmly believed that it was Fate.

"I forgot to ask how your mother is today," Molly said. The girl beside her passed a stack of sheet music. Molly took one copy and gave the stack to Louise. "Is her hand better?"

"Her fingers look awful," Louise said. "Yesterday she waited at the hospital for eight hours and still didn't get in to see a doctor, so she said she'd rather die of gangrene at home than while she's waiting in a cold room with a hundred people who are sick with all kinds of horrible stuff. I don't know how she stands the pain. Mrs. Carmichael brought over half a bottle of brandy that they'd been saving to celebrate the end of the war, and Mom is drinking it in her tea. Isn't that awful?"

"No," Molly said. "I don't blame her."

Mrs. Stone, who worked at the parachute factory, had had a terrible accident. The safety guard had been taken off her sewing machine so that she could sew faster, and she had caught her fingers under the high-powered needle and stitched four of them to the cloth before anyone had a chance to help her. Now her fingers were infected and swollen so huge that she couldn't get her hand through the sleeve of a blouse. The doctor who had cared for both the Stones and the Donnellys had been drafted years before, and so far she'd had no medical attention.

"We heard about a doctor in North Seattle who will see you in his office right away if you pay him twenty dollars up front," Louise said, lowering her voice because Mr. Prescott had come in the room.

"Twenty dollars!" Molly whispered. A doctor's office call usually costs two or three dollars. "Is she going?"

"She says she won't, but Dad wants her to."

Both girls straightened in their seats when Mr. Prescott rapped his music stand with his baton. Scowling, he told them to open their music, then he nodded at the boy sitting at the piano. Class began.

Ivy Nickerby was the best singer in class, the soloist, and the only student ever to prompt a smile from Mr. Prescott. She sat in the last row of first sopranos, where her perfect pitch could benefit the girls ahead of her.

Molly and Louise, strong second sopranos with good pitch, were expected to be of as much help to the girls sitting in front of them. But, as Louise pointed out, they were only a little bit better than the others. Consequently, Mr. Prescott found much to criticize in their section.

Of course, he found much to criticize everywhere else too. Suddenly, in the middle of a passage, he leaped off his podium and rushed down the center aisle, lunging at the tenors, smacking his baton on the nearest music stand.

"Listen to yourselves, tenors!" he yelled. Don't you ever listen? You sing like you have lace on your shorts!"

The girls in the room collapsed into giggles. Molly felt a

warm surge of pity for Paul and Henry, whose voices still cracked sometimes, especially if they were nervous. Mr. Prescott was relentless and unforgiving, and the tenor section was in trouble. Mr. Prescott threatened daily to leave them out of the spring music festival.

"Sissies!" he shouted. "You sound like girls. Scoot your chairs up and sit with them and get it over with."

Molly slid down in her seat. This was awful. Mr. Prescott's rages were awe-inspiring and hilarious if they were directed at someone else. But she found it hard to laugh when they were directed at sweet, gentle Paul and Henry.

But after class, the boys seemed to have forgotten their humiliation. They waited outside the door while Molly and Louise gathered up their books and purses, and then, to Molly's surprise, offered to walk them to their next class, algebra.

Paul walked with Molly, and Henry, stooping a little, walked beside Louise, who appeared to be too petrified to speak.

"We wondered if you girls would like to go ice-skating some Friday night," Paul said. He cleared his throat twice and looked down at his feet.

Molly glanced back at Louise, who seemed stricken, her face white.

"Ice-skating?" Molly repeated.

"You do like to skate, don't you?" Paul asked, so earnest and solemn that Molly wasn't certain if she was being asked for a date or questioned by some sort of poll-taker.

"I love to skate," Molly said. "But . . ."

Are they crazy? she thought. Louise can't skate. Doesn't he notice that she limps? She's never skated in her whole life.

"I can't go because I'm busy that night," Louise said suddenly, her voice too loud in the hall. Several students turned to stare at her.

"We didn't say which night," Henry said. He was as earnest and sober as Paul. "We can pick a time when you aren't busy."

Louise's face flushed red and her eyes glittered with tears. "I'll always be busy," she said, and she turned abruptly toward the door of the girls' lavatory.

Dismayed, Molly saw her disappear. She turned to Paul and saw that he looked as miserable as she felt.

"Louise doesn't skate," Molly said. "So if she doesn't go, neither will I."

"I'm sorry!" Paul wailed. Henry seemed incapable of speech, shoved his hands in his pockets, and studied the bulletin board with intense interest.

"Look, maybe we could do something else," Paul said. His voice cracked and his face flamed. "Henry's church is giving a dance this Friday night. We could go there."

Molly stared at him, dumbfounded. "Louise *limps*. Haven't you and Henry noticed that?"

"Oh, God," Henry groaned.

"Look," Paul began.

"Go away," Molly said. She rushed into the girls' lavatory, tears in her eyes, and her face scarlet.

Inside, Louise was watching her reflection in the mirror. "What else did they say?" she said when she saw Molly.

Molly slammed her purse and books down on the shelf under the mirror. "They wanted us to go to a church dance."

"You could go," Louise said without expression.

Molly turned to face her. "Henry really wants to take you somewhere, but they've ruined everything, and I can't see how those two dumb clucks can fix things now."

"It's Paul who wants to go out with you," Louise said loyally. "Henry and I would just be hanging around."

"Oh, who cares, who cares!" Molly cried, exasperated. "First ice-skating and then a dance. Why don't they just ask the two of us to do a jig in Victory Square in front of the Olympic Hotel? Boys are hopeless."

"No, I'm the one who's hopeless," Louise said. "Gimpy Louise, the cripple."

"Stop that!" Molly said. "Nothing is your fault. It's all *their* fault. Why are boys so tactless? They don't have any brains at all."

The second bell rang and Louise winced. "We're late to algebra."

"And I still haven't figured out if they asked us for our first date or not," Molly said. "Why does everything have to be so complicated?"

"Because there's a war on?" Louise asked, grinning.

Both girls laughed then, but Molly had difficulty concentrating on anything for the rest of the day. She had been asked out for a first date and somehow everything collapsed.

Dutifully, she recorded the entire event in her journal that evening, adding a few lines directed at Emily, who, Molly thought, would read the journal from cover to cover one day.

"Emily, remember when we wondered what it would be like to have a boy ask us for a date? Well, now I know. It doesn't seem to work out very well."

Mrs. Stone was hospitalized the following week because the infection in her hand had spread up her arm. She remained there for six weeks and came home on a March Saturday when the first daffodils bloomed in the Donnelly yard.

Recklessly, Molly picked them all and carried them to the Stones' house. Louise, ecstatic, met her at the door.

"She's lying on the couch," Louise told Molly in the hall. "Wait until she sees these daffodils! They're her favorite flower."

"I bet you're glad she's home," Molly said. The Stone family was close, closer than the Donnellys. Louise and her mother managed to stay friends, no matter what, which was more than happened between most of the mothers and daughters Molly knew.

"Come in, talk to her," Louise urged.

Molly followed behind and was shocked at what she saw. Mrs. Stone had always been overweight, but her skin and hair were beautiful, and she had luminous blue eyes shadowed with thick lashes. The woman on the couch was thin as a stick, with yellowish skin and eyes almost concealed in wrinkles. The rich, copper hair had dulled to rust and was streaked with gray.

"Molly, aren't those flowers gorgeous," Mrs. Stone said.

Molly recognized only the voice. Nothing else about the woman was familiar. Mrs. Stone stretched out her right hand, while the left, the injured one, lay on her chest.

Molly took Mrs. Stone's good hand and squeezed it lightly, trying to keep her eyes away from the other one. But she had seen the twisted fingers, the hideous scars, the discolored flesh.

"How are you feeling?" Molly asked her.

"It's wonderful to be home," Mrs. Stone said.

"And she's not going back to work, either," Louise said. "Aunt Shelley's leaving as soon as Mom can manage with just me helping her."

"I think I can say that I'm retired now," Mrs. Stone said, laughing. She covered the mutilated hand with her good one and smiled up at Molly. "I'm looking forward to being a housewife again."

Molly wondered if her own mother would make such a statement, and decided that she would not. Mrs. Donnelly operated a crane in the shipyard now. She had told Molly once that she made nearly as much money as Molly's father, even with his night-shift bonus. She wanted to learn to drive, and she was saving money for the car she planned to buy for herself as soon as the war was over and cars were available again.

"I'll never quit working," she had said more than once.

"I love it. I don't know how I stood being home all those years."

Meanwhile, Rachel, who was now a college student, supervised Dusty every school day from three until five-thirty, when Mrs. Donnelly reached home. She was forceful enough to demand his respect, although he insisted, regularly and loudly, that he hated "that big farm hick."

Rachel did her homework at the kitchen table, and Molly was so accustomed to her presence in the house that she was close to regarding her as a member of the family. It was understood by both of them that Molly might question Rachel on certain intimate things, as she would a sister.

"Rachel, have you ever had a real date?" Molly asked a few days before her fifteenth birthday. "I mean one where the boy comes to the house to pick you up and then takes you somewhere."

Rachel lifted her head and smiled. "Not like that, no."

"But you've got a boyfriend," Molly said. "I see you taking letters out of your mailbox."

"Maybe they're from a girlfriend," Rachel said, returning her concentration to her book.

"Nobody stops in the middle of the porch to read a letter from a girlfriend," Molly said. "Tell me how you got this boyfriend. I need to know."

Rachel closed her book and sighed. "You're going to keep at me, aren't you? Okay. He's not a regular boyfriend. He's somebody who used to live in Rider's Dock and worked on Grandpa's farm. We like each other a lot, but we've never been on a real date. We started writing to each other when he moved away."

Molly sat down at the table. "That's no help. You sort of accidentally slipped into having a boyfriend. I need advice on changing a regular friend into a boyfriend."

Rachel opened her book again and sighed. "Wait until you're asked. You sound like a girl who's planning on manipulating a boy into something. You might get him to do it, but he'll be sorry and then he'll make you sorry."

"I was not planning anything like that," Molly argued. "Don't make me sound like a Tent Town girl. He tried to ask me out for a date last winter."

She explained the circumstances and was annoyed by Rachel's hoot of laughter.

"That must have been something to hear," Rachel said. "I wish I could have been there. Didn't it ever occur to you that you could have said Louise didn't skate or dance and so the four of you should go to a movie instead?"

"I didn't think of it until later," Molly confessed. "By then it was too late. Paul's never even hinted at anything like that again, and I can't just come out and ask him, can I?"

Rachel considered this. "No, I guess not. I don't know why not, but the way things are, girls have to wait to be asked. But next time be ready to tell the truth right away, if he suggests something dumb like taking Louise skating again. And then come up with a substitute. Now can I get back to my homework? I'm not the newspaper lovelorn column, Molly."

Molly would have sassed Rachel, but Dusty, who had been unhappily weeding a flower bed, stuck his head in the door to announce that Rachel's grandfather had arrived at the Hawke house with a lady and a big basket of eggs.

Rachel hurried out, smiling, and Molly followed. She had seen Rachel's grandfather two or three times over the years, but had never met him. Now she lingered on the porch, watching Rachel greet the old man, then hug the fat, laughing woman who accompanied him before leading them both into the Hawke house.

"I'm tired of weeding," Dusty whined.

"Keep working," Molly said. "You know Rachel gets mad if you don't finish what you start."

"I'm not finishing it if she's not watching," Dusty argued, throwing down the hoe.

"If she looks out the window and sees that you're fooling around again, she'll snatch you bald," Molly advised.

"I'm going over to the Ts'," Dusty said and, glaring at Molly, he took one step forward, coming down hard on the hoe blade. The handle shot up and hit him square in the face.

He screamed and blood gushed from his nose. In moments, his shirt was saturated. Blood spattered everywhere, as Dusty, cradling his face, danced in agonized circles.

"What happened?" Rachel yelled from the porch next door.

"Dusty smashed himself in the face with the hoe handle," Molly shouted over Dusty's screams. "You'd better come over."

Rachel ran down the steps and across the lawn, followed by her grandfather and his friend.

"His nose is a mess!" Rachel exclaimed, after she had pulled Dusty's hands away from his face so that she could see the damage. "It looks broken."

Dusty went on bellowing, pushing Rachel's hands away when she tried to grab him.

"Quit that goddamned racket right now or I'll kick your butt!" Rachel's grandfather shouted.

Dusty stopped bawling instantly.

Rachel's grandfather was not a large man, but he grabbed Dusty and held him while the fat lady examined Dusty's face.

"What do you think, Annie?" the old man asked.

Annie turned Dusty's face one way and then the other. "Oh, his nose is busted, all right. But there's no bone in it at his age. It's all gristle."

"Can you fix it?" Rachel's grandfather asked.

"Bring him inside the house," Annie said. "Rachel, get my knitting bag out of the truck." Then she looked at Molly. "We'll need some clean towels, honey."

They led Dusty to the kitchen, and Molly ran for the towels. Rachel came in with a knitting bag, which did not contain yarn, but instead held dozens of paper packets, small jars, and twists of paper.

Annie soaked a towel in cold water and cleaned off Dusty's face. His nose was definitely crooked, leaning to one side. Both his eyes were swelling shut.

"Should I get ice?" Molly asked. "We've got ice cubes."

"They'll do in a minute or so, but first let's take care of this," Annie said, and before anyone could react, she shoved Dusty's nose back in place.

His screams must have been heard in downtown Seattle, Molly thought. Fresh blood gushed from his nose and Annie demanded ice then. Molly rushed to get the tray from the refrigerator, dumped the ice into another towel, and handed it to Annie.

The woman held the ice against Dusty's face while barking out orders to Rachel. "Get out a two-quart pan, Rachel. Fill it almost full and put it on the stove to boil. Then take that little twist of pink paper in my knitting bag—yes, that one—and empty it into the water, along with a good handful of the leaves in the jar with the blue lid. And then give me a wad of spider webs from the old jam jar. You're a good girl."

"What's all that for?" Molly asked. "Are you going to make him drink it?"

"You'd like that, wouldn't you, missy?" Annie asked. She had bright brown eyes, full of laughter. "No, I'll make a poultice. He'll have black eyes without it. And the spider webs will keep infection away from the places where his skin is scraped off."

"I don't want spider webs on my face!" Dusty screamed.

"My God, but he's noisy," Rachel's grandfather said sourly. "You have to put up with this all the time?" he asked Molly.

"Unless Rachel or my Uncle Charlie are here," Molly said.

"They smack him, do they?" the old man asked with great interest.

"It gets his attention," Molly said.

Rachel's grandfather threw back his head and laughed. "By God, you're all right, missy. What's your name?"

"Molly Donnelly," Molly said. "What's yours?"

"Abel Chance," the old man said, and he offered Molly his hand. "This here old woman is Druid Annie, my neighbor in Rider's Dock. She's part witch, some say, but she can heal people as good as any doctor ever did."

"Better," Rachel said. "She doesn't charge as much."

By the time Mrs. Donnelly came home, Dusty was lying on the couch listening to the radio, perfectly content with his invalid state. Abel Chance and Druid Annie had left, and Rachel was peeling potatoes at the sink.

The entire incident was repeated for Mrs. Donnelly's benefit, and then again for Uncle Charlie, who came home half an hour later. Dusty, thriving on the attention, settled himself at the kitchen table and displayed his swollen nose to everyone who wanted a second look.

"I'd like to thank the lady who did this," Molly's mother told Rachel. "And I think I should send her some money for her trouble."

"She always treats people the first time free," Rachel said. "The potatoes are ready to go in the pot, Mrs. Donnelly. I'd better get on home now. Mama and Rider will be there any minute."

"I don't know what we'd do without you, Rachel," Mrs. Donnelly said.

Rachel's eyes flickered toward Dusty, who frowned. "The war can't last forever," she said.

But Mama doesn't want to quit her job, Molly thought. What's going to happen then?

But she knew the answer to her question, and it filled her with bitterness.

☒ 10

June 1944

The Allies have invaded Europe to take it back from Hitler. Dad says the end of the war there is in sight, and I hope he's right. But the war with Japan is different. We seem to be fighting all alone there. No one worries about being bombed here anymore. But I can see what the war has done to Americans any day I go downtown. There are so many servicemen on hospital passes—some of them are missing a limb, and some have terrible scars. One wore an eye patch. When I think of them, I'm ashamed of being sick of rationing, sick of war talk, sick of all the changes. Emily, you've gone through so much that I don't know about. I must seem like a whining brat to you.

"Do you want to go to a movie some night?" Paul asked.

Molly, who had been pulling rubbish out of the locker she shared with Louise, cleaning it out on this last day of school, gawked at Paul.

"I mean you and Louise both, of course," Paul added. "Henry's asking her, too. All four of us could go. But Henry and I will pay." He stopped talking suddenly and swallowed.

Molly's ears rang. "You're asking me for a date?"

Paul nodded. "Yes, and Henry's asking Louise as soon as he sees her. Will you go if she does?"

Molly looked around the hall. Louise was nowhere in sight, and Molly suspected that she was still in art class, talking to her favorite teacher. Paul had caught her off guard, and she was miserably aware of her appearance—messy hair, dirty hands, and yes!—the ultimate in humiliation—the slip that Louise had left in the locker was dangling out.

"Nearly everyone else has left already," Molly said, when she finally found her voice. "If Henry doesn't find Louise, then what are you going to do?"

Paul looked at her with exasperated patience, apparently in charge now that he had seen her awkwardness and lost his own. "Molly, he'll phone her up. Isn't that all right?"

"He has her telephone number?" Molly asked, and felt stupid the moment the question popped out of her mouth.

"He got it out of the phone book," Paul explained. "He wanted to call her lots of times, but he didn't. But if he doesn't see her this afternoon, he'll call her at home. So what do you think?"

"About Henry calling Louise?" Molly asked. "I guess she'd like that."

"No, I mean about going to a movie—the four of us."

Molly gazed into his turquoise eyes and was lost, dissolving into an ecstatic laugh.

Paul's clear skin turned pink again. "You'll go?"

"Oh, I'd love to," she blurted finally. "If Louise goes, I mean. And I bet she will."

Satisfied, Paul's stiff shoulders relaxed. "Good. Say, I could help you with that. Our locker was even messier . . ."

Oh no, Molly thought in wild despair. He's seen Louise's slip.

She slammed the locker door shut and stood in front of it. "Maybe," she began, "maybe, now, maybe . . . you could call me and we could set a definite date and time."

He's changed his mind, she thought. Now that he's heard me stutter and seen Louise's slip with the torn hem, he's changed his mind and he'll never ask me on a date again, no, not ever.

"Sure, I can call you," Paul said. "Anytime you say. When?"

"I'll give you my phone number," Molly said, bending to snatch up her purse and get out paper and pencil.

"I got it out of the phone book," Paul said.

"You did?" Molly asked.

"A long time ago," Paul told her. "In eighth grade."

Then why haven't you called me? Molly wondered. Why?

Paul had left her to finish cleaning the locker when she saw Louise limping casually down the hall, as if nothing in the world could happen that was more important than the last day of school.

"Want to go to the drugstore for a Coke?" Louise asked.

"Where have you been?" Molly demanded. "Did Henry ask you to go to a movie with us?"

"Henry?" Louise asked. "What are you talking about?"

Molly explained that they had been invited out on a real date.

"I'm going to die right here," Louise said. "I can't believe it. Henry won't call. But wouldn't it be the most exciting thing that ever happened? Wouldn't it?"

Henry did call Louise—and Paul called Molly, many times—and the date was finally set. On the last Saturday in June, the boys would take the bus to the park. Paul would walk to Molly's house to pick her up, and Henry would walk to Louise's. Then the four of them would meet at the playground, take a bus downtown, and see Ingrid Bergman in *Gaslight*. After that, they would have hamburgers in a restaurant that Henry swore did not use horsemeat.

"I've got a real date," Molly told her mother, out of Dusty's hearing.

"That's nice," Mrs. Donnelly said. She was impatiently removing nails from an old board in the back yard, then straightening them by holding them carefully on a flat rock while tapping them with a hammer. "I need an extra shelf in the pantry," she said, "and there isn't a nail to be found in the entire world, I do believe."

"Did you hear me, Mama?" Molly said. "I've got a real date."

Her mother looked up, smiled briefly, and gave her attention back to her work. "I heard every word. But I already knew about it because Dusty told me."

"Dusty!" cried Molly. "How did he find out about it?"

"He listens when you talk on the phone," Mrs. Donnelly said. "You know how boys are."

Molly studied her mother for a long moment. It's as if she's a distant relative or a neighbor, she thought. Why can't she be like Mrs. Stone, who'd give Bobby something to think about if she caught him eavesdropping on Louise?

"Then I guess it's all right with you if I go to the movie with Paul," Molly said.

"Oh, sure," her mother said. She put the board aside and gathered up the nails. "Fifteen is a nice age to start dating. And Paul's a fine boy."

Rachel's reaction was more satisfactory. "You're going on a real date?" she asked, grinning over the pan of strawberries she was hulling on the back porch. "Is he in your class? Is he nice?"

"Yes and yes and yes!" Molly exclaimed. "I can hardly wait. I wish I had a new dress—Louise's mother is getting her something new—but I can wash and starch my blue cotton dress."

"I'll set your hair if you like," Rachel offered. "This is pretty exciting. It's starting out to be a summer I'll remember for a long time. Guess what? My grandpa's getting married next Saturday. How about that?"

"Is he marrying Annie?" Molly asked.

"Who else would have him?" Rachel asked, laughing.

"I'll be the maid of honor. Would you like to come? Annie asks about you all the time. She'd love to have you there. It'll be at the farm in Rider's Dock."

"They aren't being married in a church?" Molly asked, fascinated.

Rachel shook her head, laughing. "My grandpa doesn't think much of churches, and neither does Annie. So they'll have a justice of the peace come by the house."

"It's too bad your boyfriend won't be here," Molly said.

Rachel's smile faded. "Yes," she said, and she sighed.

Something was gone from the day, some light touch of happiness that had shone like sunlight on the two girls in the yard.

The war, the war, Molly thought as she turned to go back in the house.

On the night of her first date, Molly wrote this in her journal:

I've had my first real date and my first kiss, right out there on the front porch, even if Uncle Charlie did try to spoil it all by leaning out of his window and saying, "Oh, my God, why have You stuck me with a niece who doesn't know enough to go around to the back door to kiss a boy goodnight?" Paul laughed and ran down the steps, and I'm afraid that he'll never kiss me again. Maybe Uncle Charlie was trying to get back at me because we passed him on the bus tonight. He was walking out of the seminary building behind the big church on 15th. Is that where he's been going on Saturday nights for all these months? I wonder.

Emily! I've had my first date and my first kiss! What do you think of that?

On the following Saturday, Molly accompanied Rachel and her family on the Greyhound bus to Rider's Dock for Abel Chance's wedding. It was an experience Molly would not forget.

The trip took two hours. Rachel's little brother slept the entire way, while his parents murmured quietly to each other. Rachel, sitting with Molly, was more silent than usual.

"Are you nervous about being maid of honor?" Molly asked.

Rachel shook her head. "No. I'm just feeling a little down, I guess. I grew up on the farm, and I wanted to stay there all my life. But so much has changed—I don't know if my mother will ever go back. For a while some cousins were staying there, helping Grandpa, but they've moved on too. Grandpa couldn't take care of Jonah all by himself, so at least with Annie moving in, I won't have to worry about that. But still . . ."

"Who's Jonah?" Molly asked.

"A cousin," Rachel said. "You'll see. It's a big family."

And it was. The wedding guests filled the farmhouse and spilled out into the yard, laughing, talking, shouting to one another. They had come from all over the state, using precious gasoline or riding buses, to celebrate the wedding. Molly lost track of names, even though Rachel or her mother faithfully introduced her to everybody.

Jonah almost broke Molly's heart. He was an invalid, lying on a cot on the porch, nodding and smiling at everyone who came near him. He was retarded and terribly disfigured, yet everyone stopped to greet him, bending over him, kissing his misshapen head. Rachel, risking her best dress, knelt beside the cot and took one of the boy's hands in hers.

"I told you I'd be back," she said. "Has that kitty I gave you been behaving himself?"

"Kitty," Jonah said, nodding. "Kitty."

Rider made himself at home on the cot, dragging from his pockets several small treasures to show his cousin. Someone brought Jonah a drink of water and fluffed his pillows. Someone else peeled an orange for him.

Old Mr. Chance and Annie had planned that the wedding would be held inside, but so many relatives had come that there was no room for them, and so it was held outside instead. The bride and groom took their places on the porch with the justice of the peace, a man so old and feeble that Molly wondered if he would be able to get through the ceremony.

The guests grouped together in front of the house, while chickens scratched in the dirt at their feet. Annie handed her bouquet of roses to Rachel to hold, and the ceremony began.

The sun was hot, and Molly was uncomfortable, hoping

that the ceremony would not last long. The ancient man asked if there was anyone present who objected to the wedding, a standard question asked at every wedding Molly had ever attended, and one that was never answered with anything but silence.

But this time, from the back of the crowd, a voice boomed, "I object to this wedding. It is not a Christian ceremony and this man is a blasphemer and this woman is a witch!"

There was a collective gasp. A heavyset man pushed his way through the crowd, heading for the bumbling justice, who seemed to have no idea what was happening.

"What's this?" he cried over and over, his frail old hands trembling. "Who's this?"

"Pastor Woodie," someone whispered. "It's Pastor Woodie."

The stout man had reached the porch. "Abel Chance, you will not marry this witch, as God is my witness."

"I will and be damned to you, Woodie!" Mr. Chance shouted. "Get off my property, or so help me Hannah, I'll get out my gun and fix you a new bellybutton!"

Rachel's stepfather moved forward quickly and grasped Pastor Woodie by the arm, bending over him, whispering something.

Pastor Woodie tore his arm free. "Everyone, return to your homes. There will be no wedding here today."

"There *will* be a wedding, you old fart, and that's final!" Mr. Chance shouted. He scowled at the justice. "Get on with it, get on with it."

The poor old justice looked around, apparently baffled.

Once more, Mr. Hawke took Pastor Woodie's arm. He whispered urgently, and slipped his free hand into his pocket. Molly could see his hand when he withdrew it. It contained a roll of money.

Amazed, she watched while Pastor Woodie clamped his fat white fist around the money and slipped it into his own pocket. Then, scowling at Abel and Annie, he straightened his hat and fingered his thick lips as if he might speak again, but instead, he turned and pushed his way through the crowd. His car started with a roar and a blast of exhaust fumes, and he drove away.

"The goddamn circus is over," shouted Abel Chance. "Let's get on with this wedding before I change my mind."

Molly smothered her laughter with both hands and studied her feet until she was certain she could look up again without disgracing herself. The ceremony concluded, the couple was introduced to the gathering as Mr. and Mrs. Abel Chance, and everyone cheered and applauded.

Wait until I tell Uncle Charlie, Molly thought. He'll be sorry he missed this.

Later, during the reception, Rachel joined Molly in the deep shade of an old maple tree.

"What did you think of the wedding?" Rachel asked, grinning.

"It reminded me of Uncle Jimmy's wake," Molly said.

"I never understood exactly what a wake is," Rachel said.

"It's a gathering of friends and family when somebody

dies," Molly said. "Before the funeral. Everybody gets together in the same room with the coffin and they talk about the dead person, and they eat a lot of food and some of them drink too much."

"My grandpa would like that," Rachel said. "Now tell me about your uncle's wake. Were you there?"

"Oh, sure," Molly said. "Uncle Charlie said that you're never too young to enjoy a wake."

Rachel burst out laughing. "It doesn't sound like much fun."

"Parts of it were. Parts of it were horrible. Sad, you know. But most of the time people were laughing about things that my uncle had done and said. Then something really awful happened. This lady came in—nobody knew who she was—but she was all dressed up in fancy black clothes and wearing a heavy veil. She marched up to the coffin and bent over Uncle Jimmy and yelled, 'What did you do with my ruby earrings and my hat with the hummingbird on it?'"

Rachel's eyes lit up with delight. "I love this. Who was she?"

"We never found out. After she yelled at my uncle's body, she looked around at us as if we ought to know what she was talking about, and then she stomped out. I remember that her stockings were a sort of webbed stuff, with black sequined arrows pointing up."

Rachel tipped her head back and shouted with laughter. "What did the other people say?"

Molly grinned. "Well, there was this long silence, and

then my Uncle Charlie said, 'I'm here to swear that Jimmy never wore ruby earrings in his entire life, but I'm not sure about the hummingbird hat.' But then Aunt Elizabeth screamed and fainted, and Cousin Monica had a vision . . ."

"A vision?"

"Well, she's got a vocation," Molly explained, "so she has lots of visions. Anyway, the wake broke up when a cousin from New Jersey found Uncle Jimmy's gun and fired it in the front yard to celebrate, and the neighbors called the police. Our family weddings aren't nearly so exciting."

"Did you have a wake for your cousin Maureen?" Rachel asked.

Molly shook her head. "No, of course not. You can't have a wake without a body. At least, I don't think so. I never heard of one." She turned her head sharply so that Rachel would not see her sudden tears, but Rachel saw anyway and reached out a strong hand to grasp Molly's arm.

"I'm really sorry," she said.

Molly wiped her tears on the back of her hand. "I try not to think about it, but I do. Lately, more than ever. Sometimes at night I can't get to sleep for thinking about her. Wondering how she died. And I worry about Emily. She's the girl who used to live in your house."

"The Japanese girl," Rachel said.

"I think about her and what good times we had. It seems so long ago. Gee, nearly three years."

"Doesn't she write to you?" Rachel asked.

"Not after she went to the camp. Her mother didn't want her to write. She believed that people might think they were trying to spy on us because of the jobs that Dad and Uncle Charlie have, and they'd get in even more trouble."

"They'll be back and you two can catch up," Rachel said.

Molly thought of her journal and nodded. "But sometimes I'm afraid that nothing will ever be the same again."

The Hawkes, Rachel, and Molly left the reception before it was over because they had to catch the last bus leaving for Seattle. Halfway back, Molly thought that Rachel had fallen asleep in the stuffy, hot bus, because her eyes were closed and she was so quiet. But then she heard her sigh.

"You okay?" Molly asked.

Rachel opened her eyes and said, "I just remembered that I'm going to be nineteen soon. The war—all this waiting—it's eaten a hole in my life. What can I fill it with?"

"Tears," Molly said bitterly.

But she thought that a family like Rachel's would know how to wipe away someone's tears. Her own family, at least the ones under her roof, didn't even see the tears.

No, that wasn't right. Charlie saw—through his own tears.

☙ 11

August 1944

I'm glad summer is nearly over. I found a job downtown in a department store bargain basement, sometimes waiting on customers, but most of the time stocking shelves and running errands. Rachel was offered an office job, so Mama sent Dusty off to a summer camp with the Ts. The house is so peaceful without him. My father works all night, the rest of us work all day, and the housework never gets finished.

Louise is going steady with Henry now. He is crazy about her. Think of that, Emily! One of us is really going steady. I go out with Paul every Saturday, but I'm afraid it's only a habit. He's not nearly as wonderful as I thought he'd be. In fact, he's awfully boring. I get tired of listening to him talk about sports — and he gets just as tired of listening to me talk about books and music. I don't believe we are soul mates. I try to think of you, Emily, going out with boys, but I can't. Do you have dates in that camp? Darlene says that her friend Frances does. I wish your mother had let us write to each other. Now I know she was very wrong. And Emily, it's awful when we get so old we can *recognize* the mistakes our mothers make.

On the last Sunday in August, the day Dusty was supposed to return from camp, Molly told her uncle that she was leaving the house for the whole day.

Uncle Charlie looked up from the newspaper. "Where are you going?"

"This is the last Sunday before school starts," Molly said. "I thought I'd take a sort of one-day vacation by myself."

"Thinking things over, are you?" Uncle Charlie asked. "Or are you clearing out of the house in case the whirlwind arrives early?"

"Both," Molly admitted. "A month of camp won't change Dusty. And I really do want this day for something special. I'll take the bus to Woodland Park and eat my lunch, and then walk around Green Lake. I'll be back in time to help you with dinner."

"I had my heart set on chicken today. Dare I hope?"

Molly carried her breakfast plate to the sink and held it under running water. "By the time I got to the head of the line yesterday, all they had left was lunch meat and liver. I know how much you hate liver, so I bought the lunch meat.

We can make sandwiches with the tomatoes we got from Rachel's garden. And I can cook potatoes for a salad before I leave."

"Do we have eggs? I like potato salad with hard-boiled eggs in it."

"We've only got one egg, but there'll be fresh peas in the salad, too."

Charlie smiled at that. "Okay, girl, that'll do."

Molly did her best to smile too, but she was sick of their conversations about food. Everyone ought to take food for granted, she thought, instead of discussing it endlessly before every meal to see what was available in the house and what could be done with it. But she kept her opinion to herself. The last time she complained in Charlie's hearing, he reminded her that half the world would be grateful for their leftovers. He was right, of course, but Molly was also weary of feeling guilty. She would never be the saint that Charlie was, never in a million years.

And, she thought, maybe Charlie wouldn't be such a saint if he was the one who waited in the lines during his lunch breaks several times a week. Waiting in lines for anything except gas, cigarettes, and whiskey seemed to be women's work.

"I've got some news I forgot to pass on yesterday when you got home from work," Uncle Charlie said as he helped himself to another piece of toast. "Mr. Barrows won't be in my car pool anymore."

Molly burst out laughing. "I bet he got tired of running alongside the car, trying to get in the back seat without killing himself, because you're saving gas by not coming to a stop in front of his house."

"That was the least of his troubles," Uncle Charlie said, spreading margarine on his toast. "Now just look at this unsavory mess. I never could figure out why margarine has to be white. Couldn't they drop in a bit of yellow coloring so I could pretend it's butter?"

"Louise says her Mom got some that had a little capsule of yellow dye in it. You squish it around until the capsule breaks and then mix in the color."

"That's even worse," Uncle Charlie said. "Don't buy that kind. I don't like the idea of squishing capsules around in anything. Anyway, here's the news about Mr. Barrows. He's left his wife and moved into a boarding house in Ballard."

"Left his wife?" Molly had never heard of such a thing. Ordinary men didn't leave their wives and children. That only happened in movies and books.

"I notice that you didn't ask why," Uncle Charlie said.

Molly laughed. "Do I need to? But I'm still shocked. What about the Ts? He's had a whole wonderful month without them."

"But *she's* still there," Charlie said. "It's a shame, seeing a family break up."

There are a lot of ways families break up, Molly thought as she sliced bread for her picnic lunch. The Barrows are only doing it in a noisy way. We did it silently. My parents seldom see each other, and when they do, they have nothing to talk about. Dusty is wild and impossible unless he's under Rachel's thumb, and she has her own life to live. I work or go to school or wait in line or try to catch up with housework. Only Uncle Charlie is the same as he always was. Somehow, in spite of losing Maureen, Uncle Charlie stays the same.

She looked out the window at the house where the Tanaka family had once lived. Emily's family had been destroyed too. Had she ever seen her father again, after he had been arrested and taken away?

She thought of Louise, whose mother had a mangled, crippled hand. She was only another war casualty, receiving less sympathy than the wounded soldiers and sailors because her disability came as the result of the greedy supervisor, who took away the needle guard so that she could sew faster.

She remembered Mrs. Barrows's brother, who had been killed in the war while his sister bought food on the black market and hoarded coffee and sugar.

The war has been like a magnifying glass, she thought. The best and the worst of us shows up, bigger than ever. I'll tell Emily about that in my journal. Emily. Would I recognize you now?

"What do you see out the window that's so interesting?" her uncle asked.

He startled her. She looked round at him and shrugged. "I wonder about Emily sometimes," she said.

"I see," Uncle Charlie said. He turned his attention back to the paper.

Molly stared at him. How odd that he didn't say something consoling about the Tanaka family. Once he would have. He had been outraged at their internment.

But then Molly realized that he had not said anything like that since he heard about Maureen. She opened her mouth suddenly, intending to ask him if he blamed Emily's family somehow for what had happened to Maureen, but she thought better of it. If Uncle Charlie had changed, too, she would not be able to bear it. He was the mainspring of the family. Without him, they would be lost.

By the time the bus reached Green Lake, high, pale clouds swept over the sky. A light wind breathed among the willow trees, stirring the branches, whispering. The water ruffled, rocking the lily pads and reeds. Walking swiftly and smiling to herself, Molly began the three-mile trip around the lake. It had become a favorite place for her, except for the crowded swimming beaches. But those she skirted quickly, avoiding eye contact with the boys who lounged there, idle and rude on these last days of summer.

She had reached the north side of the lake, approaching the place where wild irises bloomed, when she saw a young Marine standing close to the water's edge, looking down.

Her stride broke and she stopped. What was he doing? He was alone, standing so still, watching something.

And then he turned, as if feeling her gaze upon him.

His hair and eyes were as dark as Rachel's, but his face bore such a vulnerable expression that Molly, ignoring her mother's thousand warnings about speaking to strange servicemen, said, "Is everything all right?"

He didn't smile. Instead, he looked puzzled. "Aren't there any fish in this lake?"

She walked to the water's edge and stood beside him.

"Not any more," she said. "All the fish disappeared after meat rationing began. All the ducks disappeared, too. Even the swans. It was awful, because they were so tame. They would come right up to you, to beg for bread. I guess the hunters had an easy time killing them."

The young man looked back at the lake. "I thought that if I stood here long enough, I'd see something move after a while."

Molly sighed. "There are still frogs and salamanders. I guess nobody was hungry enough for them."

He laughed a little then, and she was amazed at the transformation in his face. "You must come here a lot," he said.

"Pretty often. Is this the first time you've seen it?"

"Yes," he said. "I'm only in Seattle for a couple of days. My parents moved in with my grandparents here after I went into the service in June, and I wanted to see them before I shipped out."

"How old are you?" Molly blurted. He didn't look old enough to be in the service.

"Eighteen," he said. "Don't tell me I don't look it. That's what my sister says."

"Do they live around here?" Molly asked.

"One block away from the lake," he said. "The house is full of people — I needed to stretch my legs. Do you live here?"

"I came on the bus," Molly said. "Are you walking all the way around?"

"I will if you will," he said.

"I've gone half way," Molly said. "But come on, I'll show

you where the swans used to live. And maybe, if we're lucky, we'll see a sea gull. Sometimes they come in from the Sound, looking for treats."

He was nearly a head taller than she, but he didn't rush when he walked, as tall boys often did. "Where are you from?" she asked.

"Oregon," he said. "But I've been training in California."

"Do you know where you'll be sent, or is that the wrong question?" Molly asked.

"I don't know the answer," he said. "They never tell us anything. Look, what's your name?"

"Molly," she said. "What's yours?"

"Andrew," he told her.

"You don't look like an Andrew," she said, laughing.

"Well, you look exactly like a Molly," he said, and he laughed with her.

She would never be able to remember afterward exactly what they had talked about — books and music, certainly, and other things — but she found, after a while, that they were sitting on a bench, facing the water. The sun was a pale disk in the paler sky, slipping down in the west. The wind was colder now, chilly for August. Sunday buses were few and far between. She would have to leave soon.

"Shouldn't you be getting back to your family?" she asked. She hoped that he would say no, but he nodded instead.

"You're right. I should have headed back . . ." He looked at his watch. "I should have gone back an hour ago. I forgot about the time, Molly."

"Me too." She wrapped her arms around herself, shivering in the wind. "I have to hurry if I'm going to catch the bus."

He brushed her hair back from her forehead, a gesture so unexpected that she moved away from him.

"Sorry," he said quickly. "Sorry, Molly."

She got to her feet, uncertainly. "Well, it was nice talking to you, Andrew."

"Don't take the next bus, Molly," he said. "Stay with me for a while longer."

"I can't," she said. "I'd like to, but I can't. And your family will be worrying about you."

He grimaced, as if remembering a burden. "You're right. I don't want to let you go. Tell me your last name. Give me your phone number, and I'll call you before I leave tomorrow."

"Do you have a piece of paper and a pencil?" Molly asked. "All I've got in my pocket is a bus token."

He shook his head helplessly. "I didn't know I'd be meeting anybody like you." He looked around. "There has to be a piece of paper somewhere."

"And a pencil?" she said. "I don't think this is going to work. I really have to go now, Andrew. I can't miss the bus."

"Then tell me your number," he said. "I'll remember it. I promise."

"I'm Molly Donnelly," she said, and she gave him her phone number, twice.

He repeated it all after her, and then said, "My last name is Wright, spelled with a *W*."

"Goodbye, Andrew Wright," Molly said, weighted with a sudden sadness, one without a cure.

"I'll call you, Molly," he said, and he repeated her phone number.

She walked away quickly and glanced back once. He was watching her. She was tempted to turn and run back to him, to say something — anything! — to tell him a secret to keep for her forever. To make him promise that she would see him again.

She stopped — and he ran toward her, holding out his arms. He swung her around, laughing, and then, before she could protest — or even think of protesting — he hugged her hard enough to make her gasp.

"That's to remember me by, Molly," he said. "Now go and don't look back this time, or you might get the surprise of your life."

Molly ran away, filled with pure joy. When she reached the branch in the path that led toward the bus stop, she glanced back and did not see him.

But that's all right, she told herself. It doesn't spoil anything. Nothing can spoil this.

She knew she wouldn't dare tell anyone. Louise, with her sedate, steady romance with Henry, would be horrified. Rachel was simply too old to understand. But she could write about it in her journal and when Emily came back, decide whether or not she would leave that page intact for her friend to read.

The bus reached the corner a scant moment after Molly did, and she boarded it smiling.

For heaven's sake, Molly, she told herself, you must be out of your mind. But isn't it wonderful?

Dusty was home when she got there. He was tanned and seemed taller. When she walked in, he said, "What are we having for dinner?"

"Snake tails and shingles," Molly said promptly.

"Sounds good to me," Dusty said, surprising her. She had expected an explosion.

"Did you have a good time at camp?" she asked him.

"Sure," he said. "It beats working at the community center. I learned to paddle a canoe and all sorts of stuff."

"I'm afraid to ask if you brought home a pile of dirty laundry," Molly said as she began taking vegetables out of the refrigerator.

"I threw it down the basement steps," Dusty said.

Well, Molly thought, some things don't change.

Her mother, who had been working that Sunday, arrived home before Molly had finished the salad, to greet her son joyously. Awakened by the racket, Mr. Donnelly came downstairs in his pajamas to examine Dusty's suntan and new freckles. Uncle Charlie produced a watermelon from the basement where he had been cooling it in a laundry tub.

"We're all having dinner at the same time," he said, as Molly sliced the hard-boiled egg into the salad. "Now doesn't that make you happy, girl?"

She grinned up at him. "Yes, even if it's only an accident," she said.

For a few hours, until her father left for work, the family

sat in the kitchen and talked. After a while a thunderstorm broke out overhead, rattling the windows.

"Darn it, I have to go to work," Molly's father said. "This rain reminds me that winter's around the corner."

"Be glad you can ride the bus," Charlie said. "I'm thinking of disbanding the car pool because the tires are so thin that they're dangerous now."

"You might as well, since Dinah's husband left," Mrs. Donnelly said.

"You know about that already?" Molly asked. "Charlie only told me this morning."

Her mother laughed. "She told me when I passed her house this morning. She has an interesting slant on her problem. It's because of the Japanese, she says. If it hadn't been for people like the Tanakas spying on everybody and giving all our secrets to the Japanese, then Japan wouldn't have attacked us, and there wouldn't have been any war, and the Ts wouldn't have turned into such brats, and her husband wouldn't have left her."

"Actually," Dusty said, "he left because he's got a girl-friend named LaBelle and he moved in with her. She owns a boarding house in Ballard."

"Dusty!" Mrs. Donnelly shouted. "What a thing to say."

"Hey," Dusty said, "it's not my fault. It's not the Ts' fault, either. Their dad knew LaBelle a long time ago."

"I don't understand what's happening to people in this country," Mrs. Donnelly said.

"It's the war," her husband said.

"Mr. Barrows knew LaBelle before the — " Dusty began.

"I don't want to hear another word about it," Mrs. Donnelly cried, exasperated.

Dusty exchanged a look with Molly and grinned. "Okay," he said, raising his hands as if in surrender.

But when the two of them were climbing the stairs to their bedrooms later, he whispered to Molly that LaBelle was not bad looking, at least according to the snapshot the Ts had shown him.

"And they said that she doesn't yell much," Dusty added. "Hardly at all."

Molly stifled her laughter and shut her bedroom door.

"Good night," Dusty called through the closed door. "See you tomorrow."

Good grief, Molly thought. We should have sent Dusty to camp last year.

She got into her pajamas and sat on the edge of her bed, brushing her hair, trying not to look at the alarm clock ticking on her dresser.

I don't care if Andrew didn't call, she thought. I didn't really think he would. Probably he forgot my number.

Maybe he didn't even try to remember it.

I'll never see him again anyway.

And then she heard the phone downstairs ring.

"Molly?" her mother called up the stairs. "Are you still up? It's somebody named Andrew."

"Emily," she wrote in her journal, "I've had a day you won't believe."

12

February 1945

I have trouble remembering to write in this journal,
even though I have much to write about. Emily,
are you excited about the war news? Our army is
winning in Europe and in the Pacific. The war will
be over soon, I hope, and you'll be coming home.

Last week a Tent Town boy grabbed Mama's
purse when she got off the bus. She didn't have
much money, but the boy got her new glasses. She
says the outsiders had better leave after the war, or
Seattle will be ruined. But not all outsiders are bad.
And not everybody born here is nice. Penny Price,
who lives across the street from Daryl, says the police
have picked him up lots of times. Too bad they don't
keep him. Louise and I hate passing him anywhere,
because he says crude thing about our shapes.

Yesterday we saw a sign in a grocery store
advertising bananas. Can you believe it? Bananas!
The man would only let us have one each, and they

are very green. But think of it. They are the first bananas we've seen for years. Oh, Emily, you'd get such a kick out of Louise now. She's engaged to be engaged. Henry gave her a promise ring on her sixteenth birthday, and her mother is filling up a hope chest for her. She says she's getting married the day after she graduates from high school, and you and I will be bridesmaids. Not much is happening with Paul. I heard from a couple of girls that he's been taking somebody else for walks on Sunday afternoons. That's all right with me.

I'm still writing to Andrew. He says he's coming back to Seattle for college when the war's over. Emily, he writes me poetry. I wonder what the censor thinks of that. I've been seeing every movie musical that comes to town, and I always think of Andrew — even when Paul pays for my ticket. That makes me feel guilty, so I think I'd better tell Paul that it's time for us to say goodbye.

Emily, you'll be home soon!

Molly followed Dusty's footsteps in the snow, from the gate to the front porch. She was late getting home, and tired from trudging all the way from the store carrying two bags of groceries and her school books.

Dusty yanked open the door just as she reached it.

"Where have you been?" he shouted. "I've been waiting for hours! Aunt Bridget called and she was bawling, but she wouldn't tell me what's wrong."

Molly carried the sacks to the kitchen, with Dusty walking backward in front of her, yammering and yammering, getting in her way.

"Did you call the shipyard and leave a message for Mama?" she asked.

"They wouldn't call her to the phone!" Dusty yelled.

"Don't talk so loud." Molly complained, covering her ears. "Of course they won't call Mama to the phone. You know that. But did you leave a message for her to call during her break?"

"I forgot," Dusty said. "Well, it's almost time for her to get home, anyway. What do you suppose Bridget wants?"

Molly hung her coat on a hook by the back door. "I don't know," she said, but a seed of dread in her heart sent out cold tendrils. "Maybe it's nothing important."

"She was practically screaming," Dusty said. "She said she couldn't get hold of Uncle Francis and she needed somebody right away."

"Was she sick?" Molly asked quickly.

"No, I asked her," Dusty said. He sat at the table and picked at a place on the surface where the paint was chipped.

Molly sighed. "Help me put the groceries away."

"That's work for girls," Dusty said.

"Dusty, for heaven's sake!" Molly shouted. "Name me the work that boys are supposed to do. So far, I haven't seen you do anything, not even mow the lawn."

"There's snow on the grass," Dusty whined. "How can I mow it now? The grass doesn't even grow in winter."

Molly turned her back on him, giving up.

She had beans and canned corn and wieners for dinner. In the meat market, she had heard Mrs. Barrows tell the butcher that she had dropped by to pick up her "order." Disgustedly, Molly had watched while the butcher disappeared into the cooler and then reappeared with a large package.

Mrs. Barrows had seen Molly's angry stare. "My boys need good food," she said, her voice sharp and high. "Especially since they lost their father."

A woman standing nearby had murmured, "Awwwww, poor little tykes." Clearly, she thought Mrs. Barrows meant that Mr. Barrows was dead.

Molly thought of the black-market meat that the package contained, and said furiously, "Maybe the woman you lost your husband to serves roast beef and ham, too. Maybe she even buys it from the same crook."

At that, the butcher's face darkened. "You!" he shouted, pointing at Molly. "Get out."

Molly turned and stalked out of the shop. Now she'd done it. Her mother had warned her that arguing with people over their black-market purchases would get her nothing but trouble.

In the garish artificial light of the kitchen, the wieners she had bought in the grocery store looked even more pale and unappetizing than they had at the counter.

"Wieners again?" Uncle Charlie asked, as he came in the back door. "Good. I had them in mind on my way home."

"Aunt Bridget phoned before I got here," Molly said. "Dusty talked to her. He said she was crying, but she didn't tell him what was wrong. Maybe you'd better call."

Uncle Charlie didn't bother taking off his coat. He called his sister's house quickly and began speaking immediately, as if Bridget had been waiting by the phone.

"What's wrong?"

Molly watched Uncle Charlie as he listened. He winced and bent his head, then said, "I'm coming right over."

"What happened?" Molly asked.

"Frank Junior was killed," he said.

Molly staggered back a step, bumping into the counter. "But he isn't old enough to die!" she cried.

Frank Junior dead? Impossible. His mother had told Molly once that the boy had never even had a date before he was drafted. He'd been too shy to ask a girl to go out with him.

Uncle Charlie told Molly to give the news to her parents, and then he went out the back door, banging it behind him.

Dusty crept into the room. "Frank's dead?" he asked. "But Maureen's already dead. Nobody has two cousins die."

"Kathryn Fellows at school had two brothers die," Molly said.

She slammed the can of corn to the floor and burst into tears. "The war is nearly over!" she shouted. "*It's nearly over*. Nobody is supposed to die now!"

Emily, remember my cousin Frank? He's dead. I hate this war.

Near the end of February, after the snow had melted, the weather turned suddenly warm, and snowdrops and prim-roses bloomed everywhere. Molly and Louise took advantage of the surprising early spring and planned a Sunday afternoon on the beach.

Louise waited for Molly in the park, as she always did, sitting on a swing and pushing herself gently.

"Did you bring anything to eat?" she asked when Molly arrived.

Molly held up a sack. "Two peanut butter sandwiches and two apples."

Louise held up another sack. "Two strawberry jam sandwiches and two chocolate bars."

"I don't believe it!" Molly squealed. "Chocolate bars? Is it real chocolate?"

"Of course it is," Louise said, opening the sack and displaying two Hershey bars. "Do you think I'd bother bringing the imitation stuff? I got them yesterday afternoon. I was only in line for half an hour, too. How about that? Things must be getting better."

She fell into step with Molly and they turned toward Puget Sound. Overhead, sea gulls swooped and screamed.

"Remember when Emily used to come with us on Sundays?" Louise asked. "I was thinking about her the other day, wondering if she ever thinks of us."

Molly had never told Louise that she kept a journal, or that the journal had become more of a series of letters to Emily than a collection of essays. "I bet she does think of us," Molly said. "We'll ask her when she gets back."

"If she comes here," Louise said. "Maybe her family will go straight back to Hawaii. You know how much her mother hated Seattle. Gee, everything's so different now that Emily probably would feel really strange. We're in high school . . ."

"And you're engaged to be engaged," Molly added.

Louise laughed, pleased. "And somebody else lives in Emily's house. And there are so many strange people in the neighborhood — not just the Hawkes."

"Everything's awful now," Molly said.

"I don't think so," Louise protested. "I like the way things are — well, I don't like the war, of course. But I like being in high school, and . . ."

"And Henry!" Molly said.

"Especially Henry," Louise said. "I love making plans with my mother for the wedding, even if it is two years away. I love listening to Dad and Henry talk about building a house for us on that lot my parents own in West Seattle."

"Do you ever think about the war?" Molly asked. She bent and picked up a thin branch that had fallen from a birch tree. The wood was dry and stiff, breaking easily when she bent it.

Louise looked at her strangely. "Of course I do. I felt terrible when your cousins died. You know that. I hate watching newsreels because of all the war news."

Molly cast the branch aside. She understood, for the first time, that Louise's life was too full for her to brood over distant horrors. She was suddenly overwhelmed with envy. Why couldn't she, Molly, have a life like that, full of plans and contentment, admired and petted by an affectionate family?

Instead, she could not even lay claim to a real family. There was no comparison between the Stones and the Donnellys. The Stones sat down to meals together, with Mr. Stone at the head of the table and Mrs. Stone trotting about happily, serving expertly in spite of her mangled hand. The Donnellys ate in shifts, a few at a time, and not only because of their schedules. Except for Uncle Charlie and Molly, they seemed to have no real need to spend time together.

Actually, Molly thought, they seemed to irritate one another if they spent too much time together. They had little or nothing in common to provide material for conversation. In fact, there were a number of issues that provided material for arguments, instead.

Louise and Molly crossed the railroad tracks and turned toward the water, which was flat and calm under a pale blue sky.

"Look at the cargo ships," Louise said, pointing.

Molly looked, and abruptly began laughing. "My mother helped build them," she said. "Think of that. My mother worked on them."

"Good for her," Louise said.

But she didn't see Molly's face, rigid with her effort not to cry.

The family was vastly entertained a month later when Monica, daughter of Aunt Elizabeth, eloped with a sailor she had only known six days.

"I thought she had a vacation," Dusty said, as he sliced thick pieces of bread for his lunch.

"I think you mean *vocation*," Mrs. Donnelly corrected, laughing. It was Saturday, and she had just returned from shopping, so the counter was littered with odds and ends from the grocery store and the variety shop. "Well, that's the problem that's caused Elizabeth to take to her bed. Monica was supposed to enter the convent as a novice in June."

"Where did she meet the sailor?" Molly asked, fascinated. All the girls in the family had been forbidden even to speak to military men they had not known before the war. Her own relationship with Andrew had been tolerated, after a great deal of arguing, only because he was thousands of miles away and could do no harm to her.

Mrs. Donnelly, scowling, examined a small packet of straight pins. "That clerk swore to me that these were steel pins, but look at this, Molly. You can see where the silvery stuff has come off this pin. It's nothing but junk."

"Mama," Molly said patiently, "where did Monica meet the sailor?"

"Ah," her mother said. "Now that's what we all wonder."

"She picked him up," Dusty announced.

"We don't know that," Mrs. Donnelly said.

"But she probably did," Molly said.

"Probably," her mother said, "and I wouldn't look too pious about that, missy, considering that fellow who writes to you every five minutes."

"It's not every five minutes," Molly argued. "It's only a couple of times a month."

"Well, he ought to be concentrating on winning the war instead of writing letters to you." Mrs. Donnelly snatched up several pairs of socks and headed toward the stairs. "Molly, did you soak the whites this morning?"

"Yes," Molly said. She cut an orange into quarters and ate it at the sink, looking out into the yard where the willow tree was showing pale yellow buds. "And he is concentrating on winning the war," she added under her breath.

"'Molly, what would I have done if I hadn't met you?'" Dusty said, snickering. "That doesn't sound like a Marine. It sounds like a sissy."

Molly turned on him. "You've been reading my letters!" she yelled. Then the full significance of Dusty's quotation struck her. "You've been reading my letters and my journal!"

Dusty ran for the back door, but Molly grabbed the back of his shirt, pulling him to a halt.

He was laughing, and Molly fell on him in a rage, slapping his face and shoulders, pinching his arms.

There was a time when Dusty would have screamed for his mother, but now he only laughed, holding his arms over his face to ward off her blows.

"'You'll be a famous writer someday, Molly,'" Dusty shouted, laughing. "'Or you'll be a poet or musician or artist. And you won't even remember my name.'"

Molly grabbed his ear and twisted it until he howled. When he escaped out the door, she slammed it behind him and leaned her head against it.

I'm sick of being his mother, she thought. He's too old for a baby-sitter now and too big a brat to be left alone for long. And Mama will never quit her job. Never.

"Mama, what are you going to do when the war's over?" Molly asked that night while they were washing dishes together.

"I'll dance in the middle of the street," her mother said. "Along with everybody else."

"No, I mean what will you do about your job?"

"Keep it if I can," her mother said. "My job didn't exist before the war, so there's no serviceman who can lay claim to it. I'm hoping that the union will back me up."

Molly took a hot, wet plate from the rack and wiped it slowly, thinking out her next words with care.

"But don't you want everything to be the way it was before the war started?" she asked.

Her mother stared at her. "Of course not! Why would I want something like that? I love working. I love that paycheck. Why would I give up all that to stay home again?"

"But what about us?" Molly asked. Her mouth was numb. She was afraid of how her mother would answer this question.

"What about *you,* you mean," Mrs. Donnelly said. "It's not as if you were only three years old, Molly. Good heavens, you're old enough to run the house by yourself."

Molly could not control herself. "Why should I run it?" she shouted. "It's not my house! Dusty's not my son! Don't you know how sick I am of doing everything?"

"Everybody has to make sacrifices during a war," her

mother said. She tipped the dishpan over and drained out the water.

"But I'm talking about when the war is over," Molly said, hating herself for the tears that were stinging her eyes.

"I give you a bigger allowance than Louise gets," Mrs. Donnelly said.

"Louise doesn't do all the housework," Molly said.

"And neither do you," her mother snapped back. "I work around here all weekend to keep this place going. Don't try to accuse me of sticking you with everything."

"Dusty doesn't do anything!" Molly cried.

Her mother's mouth tightened. "Well, boys — " she began.

"And neither does Dad. He sleeps all day and works all night, and he doesn't even do yard work in the summertime."

"Charlie does most of it," Mrs. Donnelly said.

"And I do the rest."

Her mother turned on her. "What do you want from me? A promise that I'll quit my job? Well, you're not getting it."

"We aren't even a family anymore," Molly cried.

"What's a family?" her mother demanded. "You define one and I'll show you a thousand exceptions. A family is a group of people related by blood living under one roof and trying to do the best they can, that's all. Stop making yourself sick over some silly idea you got out of a movie or a book. Things are different now. A woman's a fool if she gives up a good job for housework."

Molly folded the dishtowel and hung it on the rack. She

would have left the room, but her mother grabbed her arm.

"Listen to me," her mother said, her voice softer now, urgent. "A woman has to have a way to support herself. She needs to learn to do something that will earn money, just in case. Otherwise, she's a hostage to circumstances. She can end up a widow, or separated, like Mrs. Barrows. Or even divorced. More and more women are divorcing their husbands now, instead of putting up with beatings and drunkenness and unfaithfulness."

Molly pulled her arm away. "Things weren't like that before the war."

Her mother laughed harshly. "Things have always been like that," she said. "Now we have a chance to be independent. If we don't take it, we'll be sorry. Men respect us more if they know we can walk out anytime and take care of ourselves."

"But that's . . . that's . . ." Molly bit her lip.

"It's not very romantic," her mother said. "But neither is life. Get used to the truth, Molly. It doesn't get any prettier with time."

Molly went upstairs and sat in her room with the journal and letters in her lap.

"Emily," she said aloud, "I don't even remember what you look like anymore. Maybe I wasn't writing to you after all. Maybe I was writing to myself."

She bent and put the journal in a suitcase she had brought up from the basement. Then, one by one, she put Andrew's letters beside it, closed the lid, and locked it.

She climbed the stairs to the third floor, where Charlie slept, and rapped on his door.

"Is that herself?" Charlie called out. "Or is it somebody else?"

She opened the door and carried the suitcase into Charlie's room.

"Leaving home, are we?" Charlie asked. He was sitting at his desk with a book open before him.

"Dusty's been reading my journal and my letters," she said. "Can I leave them here with you? I don't think he'd look up here, but I've locked it, just in case."

"Oh, he'll look here," Charlie said. "He goes through my things regularly."

"Why didn't you give it to him with the fly swatter?" Molly asked, outraged.

"Won't cure him," Charlie said. "Nothing cures a snoop. He'll probably grow up to be a private detective or a spy. You have to learn to put out decoys. Now if he's already read this stuff, why don't you just leave it in your room and set up something here for your new journal and letters?"

Molly shook her head. "I don't want him touching it again. He . . . he dirtied everything."

Charlie sighed. "I see what you mean. Okay, I'll stow it away in my secret place. And you can come up here and add to it whenever you want. How's that?"

Molly nodded.

Charlie knelt beside the desk, feeling along the wood paneling on the wall next to it. Molly heard a click and saw Charlie slide back a section of one panel.

She laughed. "When did you build that?"

"Oh, years ago," he said. "When young Dusty first discovered my hoard of good Irish whiskey."

Molly saw several bottles on one deep shelf in the secret cupboard, and a stack of papers on the other. Charlie lay his hand on the papers and said, "These are private. So is the whiskey, for that matter. But I know I can trust you."

He shoved the suitcase into the cupboard. "There, now," he said. He slid the panel shut, and showed her the small button that released the lock on it.

"I thought Dusty was getting better," Molly said. She sat down beside Charlie's desk. "I thought he'd figured out that he couldn't be a brat forever."

"Families are made up of brats and saints and a few people in between," Charlie said. "It's easier if you don't expect too much."

Molly made a face and got to her feet. "I guess," she said. "Well, thanks, Charlie. I'll try not to make a pest of myself coming up here."

"Be my guest," Charlie said.

When Molly reached the door, she turned back to look at him. "You didn't come home until ten tonight," she said. "Did they throw you out of the seminary?"

"Oh my God," Charlie groaned, "listen to her, will You? I don't know if she's having delusions or simply inventing things to drive me crazy. If You answer prayers, why haven't You given her a Prince Charming so that she's got something to think about besides deviling an old man like me? What's the point of all those novenas I've been making if You don't pay any attention to me?"

"Mama's thinking of inviting Mrs. Barrows to dinner tomorrow, Charlie," Molly said, laughing as she closed the door behind her. "Sweet dreams."

❦ 13

May 1945

The war in Europe is over. President Roosevelt died last month, without knowing how close victory was. On May 8 the country celebrated V-E Day, and nearly everybody I know went downtown to yell and sing and dance in the streets.

Yesterday the supermarket had roast beef, and I could have bought one for us if Dusty hadn't glued all my red-point tokens to his model airplane for decoration. Mama got mad at him for once and took away his allowance.

I've been thinking about signing up for summer school with Louise so I can graduate a year early too. She'll get married afterward. But what would I do if I finished school early?

Work at the shipyard with my mother? I'd hate that.

I haven't had a letter from Andrew for six weeks.

Molly sighed, closed her journal, and dropped it on the floor beside her. Uncle Charlie, hunched over his desk writing letters, looked up.

"What was that big sigh about?" Charlie asked. He put down his pen and turned to face her. The light from his lamp shone on his silvered, thinning hair. He was growing old too quickly.

Molly looked away. "This journal is nearly full. Remember when you told me that I should write essays about life instead of keeping a plain old diary? Well, I've almost filled this book, and I still don't understand what life is all about."

"If you did, you'd be the only person who ever lived who figured it out," Charlie said.

"I thought people in churches understood everything," Molly said. She closed her journal, put it in her suitcase, and shoved it into the secret cupboard.

Charlie laughed. "They're whistling in the dark," he said.

"You'd better not let Father O'Hara hear you," Molly said.

"Why do you think it takes me so long at confession?"

"I thought you were telling him about all your sinful ways," Molly said, grinning. But then she sobered. "Of course, maybe he thinks that wondering about things is a sin."

Charlie folded a letter and slid it into an envelope. "Can't you take a joke anymore, Molly Donnelly?"

"I guess not," she said. "I've got too much on my mind to laugh about my miseries. Listen, Charlie — tell me what to do. Should I go to summer school and pick up the rest of the credits I'll need to graduate next year, instead of in two years?"

"Why not?"

"But then what will I do?"

"Go to college, like Rachel," Charlie said.

"College costs money. Dad already told me that the money in the bank is for Dusty, after Mom buys her own car. 'Girls only end up married,' he said. Or," she added bitterly, "they end up working in the shipyard."

"Is college what you really want?" Charlie asked.

"I haven't had a chance to think about it," she told him. "All my time is taken up with what I have to do today, so I don't get a chance to plan for all the tomorrows in my life."

"Then think about them right now," Charlie said, leaning back in his chair. "Pretend you're . . . oh, say twenty-two."

"That's a million years away," Molly protested.

"It's six years away," Charlie said. "If you could do or be anything you wanted, what would it be?"

Molly sat on the bed and looked out the window at the darkening sky. "I sure wouldn't work in a factory," she said.

"Put your anger at your mother aside and answer," Charlie told her.

Molly sighed. "I love my English classes, so sometimes I think I'd like to write books. But I like art classes, too. Maybe I could do something with music. I was fooling around on the piano yesterday, and I practically cried because I've forgotten everything I ever knew — or almost. I wish I'd been taking lessons all these years. I guess it's too late now."

"Where is the law that says it's too late?" Charlie asked.

"It just is, that's all. You remember Ivy Nickerby, that girl I told you about whose mother escaped from Holland to England? Well, she'll be going to some important music school back east when she graduates. But I'm not good enough for that. Ivy's been taking piano and voice lessons for years and years from somebody who's good enough to be a teacher at the music school here."

"So you need a teacher to teach you so you can audition for another teacher?"

Molly burst out laughing. "Yes."

"It sounds as if you're making this as complicated as you can. Do you have any other careers in mind that are too complicated to consider seriously?"

"Don't make fun of me, Charlie."

"I'm not making fun. I'm trying to force you to care about yourself. Yourself and your future."

Molly got to her feet. "I'll let you know if I come up with anything. Now I'm going to iron something to wear to school tomorrow."

"Think about the future," Uncle Charlie said as she opened the door. "Don't worry about what things cost. Indulge yourself in a few daydreams and let me know what you decide. Okay?"

"Okay," Molly told him. "But we're both wasting our time. In six years I'll still be here, waiting on Dusty and Dad."

"No, you won't. Change is a law of life."

"Ugly change is a law of life," Molly corrected as she closed the door.

The next day, walking home from school, she convinced herself that she could get through the front door without checking the mailbox for a letter from Andrew.

He's forgotten about me, she told herself. He's writing to a dozen other girls and he likes them better than he likes me.

Yes, that's it, she thought. I bore him, exactly the way Paul bored me. Maybe I'm being punished because I told Paul that he shouldn't waste money taking me to movies anymore because I'll never like him any better than I do now, which isn't much.

Oh, God, please let it be true that Andrew doesn't write because he doesn't like me and not because he's dead.

She climbed the porch steps, eyes averted from the mailbox, and turned the door knob. Then, frantically, she whirled and opened the box. Inside she found a late birthday card, sent to her by Aunt Elizabeth, according to the return address.

It's all right, she told herself. No reason to worry. Andrew's been writing to somebody else, somebody prettier, somebody older who's in college and planning to be a dress designer or an actress or something exciting like that.

She heard a car engine and, curious, turned back to the street. A taxi, a rare sight, slowed and stopped in front of the Hawke house. A soldier got out, slowly, as if moving hurt him. He paid the driver and then looked up at Rachel's house.

Molly had never seen him before. She was embarrassed by her own curiosity, but she could not help but watch. The taxi drove away, and still the young soldier stood on the parking strip and looked at Rachel's house.

Maybe he came to the wrong address, Molly thought.

"Can I help you?" she called out.

The soldier glanced over at her. "I'm here to see the Chance family," he said.

Molly hurried down the steps. "They don't live here," she said. "They live in Rider's Dock. That's a long way from here."

The soldier stared at her. "This is the address I have."

Then Molly understood. "You're looking for Rachel!" she cried. "She lives here. But her stepfather's name is Hawke."

The soldier shook his head, laughing at himself. "I know that," he said. "I guess I got too excited and said the wrong thing." He moved toward Rachel's house cautiously, as if he were afraid he might stumble on the rough grass.

"I'm sure Rachel's home," Molly called out to him. "She usually gets home about fifteen minutes before I — "

"Hank!" Rachel screamed. "My God, it's you. It's you!"

Rachel ran down her steps and then stopped in front of the soldier. "Oh, you're worse than you said. Why didn't you tell me?" She held out her arms and the soldier walked into them and sagged against her. Molly thought that she heard him sob.

Tears stung Molly's eyes, and she turned away abruptly. It's the boy Rachel's been waiting for all these years, she thought. He's been hurt, and she never said one word to us about it. She's so strong. She's the one they all depend on, and now the soldier will depend on her, too.

Molly shut the door behind her and sat down on the couch.

Andrew, are you all right?

I hardly know him, she thought. I only saw him once. He doesn't mean to me what that soldier means to Rachel. He's only a boy I saw one afternoon, and I'll never see him again.

The day dragged on endlessly. Dusty came home with the Ts, clamoring for sandwiches and milk. They left the kitchen a mess and tore out, heading for the Barrows's house, where Dusty had been invited to share a meal of hamburgers.

"Go ahead, see if I care," Molly cried, exasperated. She took the meat loaf she had prepared from the refrigerator and slid it in the oven. Dusty loved meat loaf, so he'd be furious when he found out that he'd missed it.

Her mother came home a few minutes early, lucky to have found a ride instead of crowding on the bus. Charlie was late, because he'd stopped for real ice cream.

"I wish I could have found it last week for your birthday," he told Molly.

"Save some for Dusty," Mrs. Donnelly told Molly. "And save some of that meat loaf for your father. He can take it to work tonight for his dinner."

Molly set the table and made a salad out of cabbage and carrots. It was too early for Rachel's garden to produce lettuce and tomatoes.

The phone rang twice. The first time it was Bridget calling Molly's mother to tell her that their car had broken down on the highway and could not be fixed. The second call came from Louise, apologizing for not being able to go to the library with Molly.

"My dad's sick and Mother needs me to help out," she said. "He's caught a terrible cold and can't stop coughing. Mother's called that doctor in North Seattle, but he won't come to the house unless we pay him thirty dollars before he even looks at Dad. Isn't that awful?"

"Is your mother going to pay?" Molly asked.

"Of course she is," Louise said. "But doesn't it make you wish you believed in faith healing?"

"It makes me wish I knew Rachel's grandmother's phone number," Molly said. "Well, I'm going to the library by myself, then. I've got a book that's due. See you tomorrow."

She took the long way back from the library so that she had an excuse to walk through the small park. Once out of reach of the streetlights, she had to find the path by the moonlight filtering through new spring leaves. She heard the distant shout of Dusty and the Ts, playing ball in the street on the other side of the park. Brats. She would collect them as she passed and make them go home.

"Well, look what we found," someone said.

She recognized the voice. Daryl Arthur. He stepped out

from behind the privet hedge that separated the path from the playground. Someone else — she thought he was from Tent Town — moved behind her and jumped forward to crowd her on the other side.

"Hello, Daryl," Molly said. She hurried toward the light she could see shining on the asphalt path at the other side of the park and toward the distant voices of Dusty and the Ts.

Daryl had grown heavy, almost fat, and looked older than sixteen. Molly could smell his sweat and the rank odor of whiskey. School gossip declared that he graduated from mischief-making to crime. He had stolen cars, some said. He had vandalized houses when the owners were away. Molly rarely saw him during the day, for he no longer bothered much with school. But she had seen him at night, hanging out on street corners with a gang of boys, smoking, taunting passers-by.

"What's your hurry?" Daryl asked. He grabbed her arm above the elbow, slowing her down.

She tried to yank her arm free, but he tightened his grasp and pulled her off the path.

"Stop it!" she cried. "Let go of me!"

The stranger grabbed her other arm. Together, they pulled her off her feet, dragging her across the grass.

"No!" she shouted. "You let go of me! Stop it!"

Daryl kicked her ribs, knocking the breath out of her.

They're going to kill me, she thought.

"Help me!" she cried, but she was afraid that no one could hear her now, for she couldn't pull in enough air to draw a good breath. "Dusty! Help me!"

Daryl pushed her to the ground, knelt on her, and jammed his hand against her mouth and nose. The other boy held her arms.

She kicked desperately, but could not free herself from their grasp. Daryl was suffocating her.

She heard a dim tangle of sounds, as if she lay underwater. Shouts, a scream, the sickening thuds of repeated blows.

She could breathe again. She sucked in sweet evening air and rolled onto her stomach, wincing from pain.

"Get up!" Dusty yelled. "You've got to get up and run!"

Her brother and the Ts hauled her to her feet and dragged her toward the path.

"Are they coming back?" Tim asked.

"I don't see them," his brother said, his voice cracking with excitement. "If they do, I'll give it to 'em with the bat again."

"Jeez, I think you broke open his head," Dusty said. "I hope you did, anyway."

They had her out on the street now, but they would not let go of her, would not let her stop to rest. Through a haze of pain and fright, she saw her house.

"Go home," Dusty told the Ts. "Don't say anything about this. If my uncle finds out we were playing outside in the dark, he'll kill me for sure this time."

The Ts ran off, their sneakers padding quietly in the street.

"Now listen to me," Dusty said, shaking Molly's arm. "Now you just *listen* to me."

Molly sagged toward the bottom step, but Dusty would

not let her alone. "You don't say anything to anybody! I was supposed to be at the Ts and they were supposed to be at our house. If you tell what happened, I'll get in trouble with Charlie again."

"I'm going to call the police! Daryl and that other boy tried . . . tried . . ."

"I don't care what they tried!" Dusty growled. "It was your own fault. What were you doing in the park this late? You were just asking for it, and if Mom and Dad find out where you were, you'll be sorry."

"I wasn't asking for anything!" Molly wept. "Are you crazy? I've got a right to walk in the park if I want to."

"No, Daryl's got a right to grab any girl he can find," Dusty said. "Are you stupid? That's how things are, Molly. If you didn't read so many dumb books, you'd know a few things."

"Leave me alone," Molly said, and she pushed him away. "You get away from me."

Dusty straightened up. "Are you coming in?"

"In a minute," she said. "Let me sit and rest. Don't tell them I'm out here yet."

"Are you kidding?" Dusty said. "I haven't seen you. I just got home from the Ts. I don't know anything about anything."

And with that, he ran up the rest of the steps and through the front door, slamming it behind him.

Molly tried to lean back, but every movement hurt her ribs. Slowly, she forced herself to her feet.

This wasn't my fault, she thought. I didn't do anything

wrong. Daryl and that other boy should be in jail. They ought to be dead!

But I'll get blamed for this if I tell. Dusty's right about that. She remembered the vague rumors she'd heard at school about one of the senior girls who got caught walking home late from the bus stop. Everybody said she'd been asking for it, being out so late alone.

Molly shook with rage. I'll be blamed! Somehow I'll pay Daryl back for this. He had no right to hurt me.

She straightened her back and climbed the steps, biting her lip to keep from groaning. When she opened the door, she heard the radio playing and her mother and Charlie laughing in the living room. She walked down the hall toward the stairs.

"I'm back, Mama," she called out. "Good night, everybody."

They answered her distractedly, intent on the program.

Carefully, she climbed the stairs. It occurred to her that if her ribs were broken, she would have to tell somebody something.

She undressed in the bathroom and studied herself in the mirror. There was a thick, blue welt over her ribs, and when she pressed it, she could hardly breathe because of the pain.

I'll live through this, she thought. I'll live through it and try to get even and never let anybody treat me like that again.

And then, as she covered herself with the old robe she found hanging on the back of the door, she understood something her mother had been trying to tell her for a long time.

The only real power that women have is the power that comes from earning their own money, she thought. Money wouldn't save her from boys like Daryl and his friend. But it would get her respect when she set out to get even.

So you're wrong, Dusty, she thought as she crept to her room. I've learned that much from the books I've read.

Two hours later she walked up the steps to Charlie's room and knocked.

"Is it herself?" he asked. "Come in, Molly Donnelly."

She opened the door and tried to smile. "I made up my mind. I want to go to college. I'm signing up for summer school so that I can start a year early. Now all I have to do is get the money, but if I find a Saturday job and baby-sit . . ."

Uncle Charlie opened the secret cupboard and drew out a brown envelope. "Have a look at this, young lady."

She opened the envelope and pulled out a bank deposit book. It bore her name.

"Charlie," she said. "What's this?"

"It's for college or a trip to Ireland or anything else you want."

She looked inside the book and blinked. "So much?"

He made a gesture of dismissal. "I only had one child. Maureen convinced me that college was important for girls. I couldn't persuade your father — well, he had more people dependent on him than I did, and saving never did come naturally to some of the Donnellys. But I think your mother's beginning to understand a few things."

Molly nodded. "But I don't think she'll understand this."

"You'll need it all — tuition, books, dormitory fees."

She raised her head. "Dormitory fees?"

"Don't stay home," Charlie said. His eyes had an odd, shuttered look. "The war's almost over. Things will change, but it won't have anything to do with you. Get on with your own life as soon as you can."

"What do you mean, things will change? Haven't we had enough changes?"

But the odd look was gone. Charlie laughed and took the envelope back. "I'll keep it here. Don't say anything to anybody for now. There's no sense in playing with fire."

"Charlie," Molly said. "Thank you."

He knelt in front of his cupboard. "When you're rich and famous, you can send me your autograph. That'll be all the thanks I'll ever need."

She turned and reached for the door. "See you in the morning," she said.

"Sweet dreams," he said.

Not very likely, Molly thought as she made her painful way down the stairs.

Two days later she received four letters from Andrew, dated a week apart. He was well, he said in one letter. The censor blacked out what came next. The last letter expressed his hope that the war in the Pacific would end before summer was over.

She answered him immediately and recorded in her journal that she had heard from him again.

And then she described the attack, in careful detail.

"There, Emily," she concluded. "I hope nothing that awful has ever happened to you."

The following day she told her parents and Charlie about it.

"It wasn't my fault," she said. Her fists were clenched so hard that her nails cut into her palms. "It was *their* fault. And someday, some way, I'll make them sorry."

"Now listen here, young lady," her father said. "You put yourself in a position for something like that to happen to you."

"No," she said. "They're in a position for something bad to happen to them because of what *they* did."

"Don't go around talking about this," her mother warned. "You know what people will say about you."

"I know what I'll say about *them*!" Molly shouted. "I have a right to my own story."

"Of course you do!" Charlie said sharply.

Charlie left the house late, after Molly and her parents had worn themselves out arguing about whether or not the boys who rescued her would talk about her. She had identified them only as a couple of strangers.

The next day Molly learned at school that Daryl had been seen with a black eye and a split lip.

She confronted Charlie in the kitchen that night when

they were alone. "You don't need to fight my battles," she said.

"I'm your uncle. I wanted to make sure he wouldn't bother you again."

"I won't give him the chance," Molly said. "I bet I'm faster than he is, and I know I'm smarter."

✄ 14

August 1945

The war is over. The newspapers say we dropped
two "atom bombs" on Japan, and so they surren-
dered. On V-J Day, Louise, Henry, and I went downtown and watched the crowds. The cars and buses
on the streets couldn't move, but nobody minded. It's
all over, Emily. You can come home now.

"So are you getting married, Rachel?" Molly asked.

She and Rachel had met on the bus and were walking
home together. Long, hot shadows fell across the quiet
street. A sprinkler hissed on one lawn, sending a sparkling
arch of water swinging over a wilted rose bed.

"Someday, I suppose," Rachel said, smiling. Then she
laughed. "Actually, we're getting married soon. Hank
wants to go to agricultural college, and we won't be separated again. I'll change schools. Everything will work out."

"Everything always works out for you," Molly said.

"You're doing pretty well yourself," Rachel told her.
"Starting your senior year already. Good for you."

They parted at Rachel's walk. "But you don't have to watch for letters anymore," Molly said.

Rachel laughed. "You and your mystery boyfriend."

Molly ran up her steps. A mystery boyfriend, especially one who was far away, had certain advantages over one who was in town. For one thing, he couldn't do much to spoil her daydreams.

She took the laundry in from the line, inhaling the fresh fragrance, smiling to herself. Without waiting to fold the clothes, she grabbed up a bowl and hurried outside again. Rachel's tomato plants were loaded. The Donnellys had big salads every night.

She heard a car door slam in the street. It was too early for anyone in the family to come home. Molly left the bowl on the back porch and walked down the driveway.

A dusty black car sat at the curb, and three people, Japanese, stood on the parking strip, looking at the house.

The man was old, stooped, leaning heavily on a cane. The woman's hair was nearly white, pulled back tightly into a skimpy bun. The girl, around twelve, saw Molly coming and stared haughtily.

The girl.

"Emily," Molly said. Goosebumps sprang up on her arms.

"Oh, Emily, you've come back!" she cried.

But the girl's lips turned down in an expression that Emily never wore.

It was Nancy Tanaka, of course! Emily would be sixteen, a young woman.

"I'm so glad to see you, Nancy," Molly said. She smiled

at the man and woman. "How are you? My parents aren't home now, but I know they'd want you to wait. Can you? They'll be so glad . . ."

"We can't wait," Nancy began.

Her father interrupted. "We have only a little time," he said. "And many people to see. Tomorrow we leave for our home. But we wanted to say goodbye to you before we go back to Hawaii, and give you something from Emily."

"Where is she?" Molly asked, bewildered.

Mr. Tanaka held out a small package wrapped in soft, crumpled brown paper.

"Emily is dead," he said. She died two months after we left Seattle, of pneumonia. She told us to give you this."

Molly took the box in numb fingers. "She's dead? Dead?"

Mr. Tanaka bowed slightly, supporting himself on his cane. "Tell your family that we said goodbye."

And then they turned toward the car.

"Wait," Molly said. "You can't go like this. Wait."

But they did not say another word. They got into the car and drove away.

The sprinkler up the street hissed and sighed. Somewhere a bird trilled and fell silent. A door slammed across the street.

Molly looked down at the small package. "But then what was the point of it all?" she said aloud. "What was the point?"

Molly opened the package on the back porch. She lifted the lid of a discolored cardboard box and carefully unfolded the tissue inside. Emily had given her a string of tiny, green shells.

There was a small card in the box. "Merry Christmas," it said. "To Molly from Emily."

This was what Emily's auntie in Pearl Harbor had sent her for Molly's Christmas gift in 1941.

Molly took it to her bedroom and closed the door, then pulled open the bottom drawer of her dresser. The beads and embroidered blouse that Maureen had sent so many years before waited there.

She sat on her bed, holding her gifts in her lap.

"What was it all for?" she asked.

On the last day of August, Mrs. Donnelly lost her job. The shipyard was laying off hundreds of workers, and the women were first to go.

Weeping furiously, Mrs. Donnelly slammed cupboard doors in the kitchen while she prepared dinner.

"I might as well get used to it," she said. "I'll never find another job as good as that one."

Molly's father, transferred back to day shift again, at a job that paid less than before, poured coffee for himself from the pot on the back of the stove. "The war's over," he said. "The country doesn't need you anymore."

"*I* need me," Mama said. She filled a pan with water and shoved it across the counter. "Haven't you cut those beans yet, Molly?"

"All done," Molly said, dumping a bowl of string beans in the pan. "What are you going to do, Mama?"

"Start looking for something else tomorrow."

Her father left the room. Mama looked after him and sighed. "We're used to the extra money," she told Molly.

"But you've got lots saved," Molly said.

"That's for my car," her mother said. "And for Dusty, when he needs it." She pulled open the pantry door, avoiding Molly's eyes.

"You'll find a new job, Mama," Molly said. She put a lid on the beans and turned up the heat. I hope, she thought.

Autumn came, with unusual storms that ripped leaves off trees before they turned yellow. Out of desperation, Mrs. Donnelly took a job with the same factory where Mrs. Stone had made parachutes. But the women at the sewing machines were making dresses now. She hated it, but it was better than poking around the house all day, she said.

Molly didn't argue when the task of grocery shopping fell to her again. There was more to buy in the stores now.

She came home with a special treat one afternoon. The butcher had steaks. They were expensive, but Molly was certain that her mother would approve.

Charlie's car was in the driveway, which surprised her.

"Charlie?" she called out when she walked in the door.

He sat in the kitchen, sipping coffee and reading the paper.

"I hope you're not sick," Molly said as she put the steaks in the refrigerator.

"Never felt better in my life," Charlie said. He folded

the paper and put it aside. "I'm glad you're home first. I've got something to tell you."

Molly pulled out a chair and sat down. "Am I going to like this or hate it?" she said.

He smiled. "For my sake, Molly Donnelly, don't argue with me. Okay?"

She nodded, chilled.

"I'm going away," he said. "There's a lot of work to be done in Europe. It's been nearly destroyed—cities in ruins, no food or medicine, refugees everywhere. The church needs men to help out."

Molly swallowed. "You're not going to be a priest, are you?"

He laughed. "Me? Now that's a thought. But I don't think the church is ready for that. No, I'm going as a volunteer."

"I thought maybe—well, I've known for years where you go on Saturday nights. To that seminary. I thought . . ."

Charlie looked out the kitchen window. "I've been struggling with a few things, hard things. Things I haven't much liked about myself. There's an old priest there who puts up with me."

"A spiritual adviser," Molly said.

"Yes."

Molly laughed shakily. "Well, thank goodness you don't have a vocation. I don't think this family can go through that again. If all you have in mind is a big penance for your sins . . ."

She stopped, seeing the look on his face.

"Charlie," she said. "What did you ever do that was so bad?"

He would not look at her. "I'll be needing forgiveness someday," he said. "But I can't seem to forgive."

"What are you talking about?"

He sighed. "The men who killed my girl might still be alive," he said. "But dead or alive, I hate them. I'm afraid I'll hate them until I die. When those bombs dropped in Japan, I was glad."

"Charlie, everybody was glad. It meant the war would end."

"I didn't think about that. I was hoping that their daughters were dying."

"Nobody can blame you for that," Molly said.

"I blame me," Charlie said. "But I can't seem to get past my hatred. Sometimes my anger is out of control—I *wanted* to hurt that fellow who attacked you. If I was a good man, I'd volunteer to go to Japan and help out. But I can't. So I'm doing what I can."

"Have you told Mama and Dad?"

He shook his head. "No, I wanted you to know first. I'll be leaving in a week. I've quit my job and cleaned out our secret cupboard, except for the things that belong to you. Don't show that bank book to anybody. You've got to promise me that right now. If you think there's a chance that you'll start feeling sorry for anybody and give the money away, then I'll take it back and give it to the church. Do I have your word that you'll keep it a secret and use it for yourself?"

"I promise, Charlie," she said. "But look here—you just look here a minute. What am I going to do if you leave? You're what holds us together. Without you, there won't be a family."

"Listen to me, Molly Donnelly," Charlie said. "Every family is like this one. There's always one person who ends up holding it together. When I go, it'll be you. But believe me when I tell you that when *you* leave—and Molly, you must!—someone else will step in. And it doesn't make any difference which one it is. It's tradition, the rituals that build up over the years, that serves as a kind of gravity. The one who presides over the rituals is the one everyone counts on. The only danger comes when that person thinks he's indispensable."

Molly wept, reaching for his hands. "Charlie, I can't do it. I'm not strong enough."

"You don't have to be strong," he said, squeezing her hands in his. "You only have to be kind for an hour at a time."

The Donnellys had a fine going-away party for Charlie. It was short notice to call all of them together, but, in addition to the family in Washington and Oregon, a dozen came from California—Donnellys no one had seen since before the war. The notorious, wild cousin from New Jersey arrived two hours after the party in the church hall began, and, as Molly explained to Louise later, he added a memorable touch.

"I wish you could have been there," Molly said, leaning

over the soda fountain table and laughing. "He was drunk before he got there, but he grabbed a pitcher of wine away from Father O'Hara and drank straight out of it. My Aunt Bridget says to the priest, 'I want you to know, Father, that he doesn't ordinarily drink right out of a pitcher,' and Father O'Hara says, 'No, dear, I'm sure he doesn't, but I do.'"

She stopped to taste her hot chocolate. "We'd all been hoping that Father O'Hara would keep the peace, but he didn't. He only made things worse. I guess he was missing Charlie already. Anyway, Mrs. Barrows was in the church, fiddling around with the side altar decoration for mass the next morning, but really she'd only come to spy on everybody. She heard all the racket, and saw my cousin drinking out of the wine pitcher and Father O'Hara dancing with Darlene, so she called the police. I don't know what she thought they'd do, especially since both the night cops in this neighborhood are members of the parish and Irish to boot. They told her to never mind, and both of them came back to the party when they got off duty, to take Charlie to the train. Father O'Hara had promised to do it, but he tripped over a chair and sprained his ankle."

"You ought to write all this down," Louise said, wiping her eyes. "Honestly, Molly, your family belongs in a book."

Molly licked whipped cream off her spoon. "Who'd want to read about the Donnellys?"

"Mrs. Parsons told the class that you write so well you could be an author someday."

Molly grinned and got to her feet. "Sure," she said. "And

I could also be a lawyer or a doctor or a . . . crane operator in a factory. But I like the idea of writing books. Are you done? I've got to start dinner early today. We're having fried chicken."

It was Louise's turn to pay the check. They waited while the new clerk, a young man, made change, and then they left together.

A few snowflakes drifted down, and Molly held her face up to them, catching some on her tongue.

"See you tomorrow," she told Louise. "Tell Henry he'd better work harder in chemistry if he wants to graduate with you and not be the only husband in high school."

Snow fell harder now, and the neighborhood was silent under the weight of it. Rider Hawke, crossing the street from a neighbor's house, waved to her. His new puppy, sassy and fat, bounced at Molly, barking. Rider grabbed him up and carried him inside.

Molly turned up her own walk. As she unlocked the front door, she heard the phone ringing and hurried to answer it.

"Hello, Molly?" she heard.

"Yes, this is Molly," she said.

"This is Andrew."

She sat down abruptly on the chair next to the phone. "Andrew," she said. "Andrew."

He laughed joyously. "I walked in on my family five minutes ago. I wanted to surprise everybody."

Molly grinned and held the phone tightly in both hands. "There'll be swans on the lake next spring."

"We aren't going to wait until then, Molly," Andrew said. "I wish you could see the lake in the snow. I'm looking at it out my grandparents' living room window. Could I come and get you?"

She shut her eyes, imagining the lake and the snow falling on the reeds and willows. "Yes. I'll be waiting."

She left a note for her mother on the kitchen table, dressed in her warmest clothes, and stepped out into the silvered twilight.

A small avalanche of snow dropped suddenly from the roof of the Hawkes' house, where Emily had once lived. Molly remembered her friend's first winter in Seattle, when she wasn't sure if she liked cold weather.

So long ago, Molly thought, looking over at the porch where they had stood together and watched the snow fall. Two little girls in caps and mittens.

Headlights turned the corner at the end of the block. Molly walked out to the curb to wait.